S0-AWG-257

I HUNGER FOR YOU
USA Today bestseller

"Sizemore's sizzling series gets more intriguing. . . . Hot romance and intense passions fuel this book and make it a memorable read."

—*Romantic Times*

"An alluring plot, page-turning excitement, and scrumptious romance."

—Romance Reviews Today

"Sizemore's vampire world is among the best . . . out there. . . . This is one book that belongs on your list of keepers."

—Huntress Reviews

"Plenty of vampires, sexual tension, and action to go around."

—A Romance Review

I THIRST FOR YOU

"Passion, betrayal, and fast-paced action abound in this sizzling tale. . . ."

—*Library Journal*

"Edge-of-your-seat thrills combine with hot romance and great vampire lore!"

—*Romantic Times*

"An action-packed, suspenseful roller-coaster ride that never slows. [Readers] will root for this passionate couple. Don't miss it!"

—Romance Reviews Today

I BURN FOR YOU

Also by Susan Sizemore

Primal Desires

SUSAN SIZEMORE

POCKET STAR BOOKS
New York   London   Toronto   Sydney

Pocket Star Books
A Division of Simon & Schuster, Inc.
1230 Avenue of the Americas
New York, NY 10020

First Pocket Star Books paperback edition September 2007

POCKET STAR BOOKS and colophon are registered trademarks of Simon & Schuster, Inc.

For information about special discounts for bulk purchases, please contact Simon & Schuster Special Sales at 1-800-456-6798 or business@simonandschuster.com.

Cover design by Lisa Litwack
Cover art by Franco Accornero

Manufactured in the United States of America

10 9 8 7 6 5 4 3 2

ISBN-13: 978-1-4165-1336-0
ISBN-10:   1-4165-1336-1

Dedicated to the
fond memory of Fern Anderson

Prologue

Central Europe, Winter 1943

Jason Cage enjoyed the company of wolves, but the trio of creatures surrounding him in the clearing had to be werewolves. No wolf had ever looked at him out of glowing gold eyes with intelligence that rivaled his own. Being surrounded by members of the Gestapo wouldn't have surprised him, nor a touch on his shoulder from the vampire Prime who also hunted him. But this pack was the last thing Jason had expected to find in the deep forest tonight.

Then again, the moon was full, the woods were remote. If he were a werewolf, he'd consider this countryside perfect for running free. Freedom was a thing every creature desired, be it mortal or otherwise evolved.

"Good evening," he said, mostly because it

was something he'd heard a vampire say in an American movie.

He hoped the largest werewolf's answering snarl was a form of laughter.

"I mean no harm to you," he went on.

He spoke calmly, without making any effort to reach the minds of the werewolves telepathically—mostly out of politeness, but also because every time he tried psychic communication lately, the other Prime somehow focused in on his use of mental energy.

The werewolves circled him, silver moonlight outlining their dark shapes. In morphed form they must be huge men, *he thought*.

It occurred to him that they *meant* him harm, which was not generally the way it went between werewolves and vampires.

"Why?" he asked as the trio drew closer.

They began to circle, growing one step nearer with each turn around the clearing. Clearly this was a dance, a ritual. Was there meant to be a sacrifice at the end?

While his ancestors might have participated in such Old Religion nonsense, Jason was a Prime of the twentieth century.

"There's a war on, you know," he reminded the circling beasts. "We should be fighting the Germans instead of each other."

They continued to come toward him.

He'd done his best to be civilized.

He smiled, happily anticipating the fight. "Very well, then."

As if his words were a signal, the pack let out an eerie howl and they all rushed him at once.

Jason laughed, tossing them around as though they were stuffed toys rather than creatures of hard muscle, sharp claws, and wicked fangs. They got in a few scratches, and a nip or two, but vampire skin was tough and healed quickly.

All in all, Jason enjoyed the game. He'd been running and hiding too much of late; this was a chance to take out his frustrations in a perfectly Primal way.

When it was finished, Jason hadn't broken a sweat and the werewolves lay in panting, exhausted heaps in the clearing. Jason was tempted to raise his head and howl at the moon himself.

What stopped him was the sudden awareness that he and the werewolves were not alone. There was a mortal standing behind him, and as Jason turned to face him the mortal began to clap.

"I'm glad you found us entertaining," Jason said to the white-bearded old man.

The mortal was shabbily dressed, but he had the bearing of an ancient prince. He lowered his gnarled hands to his side and gave Jason a regal nod. The werewolves dragged themselves from the ground and came to crouch at the old man's feet.

"Welcome, Prime." The mortal touched a werewolf's head and it leaned against his thigh. "You have done well tonight."

And it occurred to Jason that he had just been through some sort of test. But what was it, and why?

Chapter One

*O*ne more show, and then two months off—I can hardly wait!"

Jason understood his assistant's enthusiasm as they waited backstage. During their hiatus, she was going to get married and honeymoon on Bora-Bora. He had no particular plans or destination in mind.

Or he hadn't until a few minutes ago.

"Of course, I'll miss the critters. Do you think they'll miss us?"

The tigers and lions they used in the Beast Master magic show were going to be spending their holiday at a very exclusive private nature reserve. The wolves, of course, never left his side.

"They won't want to come back to work after two months of running free," Jason answered.

He fingered the talisman he'd put in his vest pocket. He'd recognized the gold coin instantly, even though only half of it had been sent to him.

Out front, the applause was beginning.

Even with his powers, it was never wise to be distracted during a performance. He wished he hadn't opened the padded envelope until he was alone in his dressing room after the show. He certainly wished he hadn't read the note.

Now he had somewhere he absolutely needed to be, and an obligation he could not refuse to fulfill.

But at this moment, the lure of the audience called him.

Northeast of San Diego, Spring, Present Day

Sofia Hunyara was aware of the weight of the pendant resting at the base of her throat. Nothing else felt like gold. It was heavy and rich, and *there* whether she could see it or not. The crescent-shaped half of an ancient coin, which she wore on a leather cord, was tucked discreetly beneath her blouse. She traced the coin's outline beneath the soft silk. Once upon a time the coin had been all she'd had, and she'd fought hard to keep it. In the last few years, she'd kept it in a safety deposit box and hadn't thought about it much—not until the message arrived last week.

She peered out of her windshield at the house on the hilltop and shook her head. The impressive mansion looked completely out of place in the California desert.

Why am I doing this? she asked herself yet again.

Probably because of her grandfather, and her great-grandfather.

She pressed her palm against the pendant.

And the fact that, except for a distant cousin, she was alone in the world and the world did not make sense. At least the past didn't make sense.

"This should go to your father," her grandfather had said, handing her a small leather bag. "I am so sorry this burden must go to you."

She tugged the bag open and spilled its contents into her cupped hand. It was what she expected, yet different. She looked at the dying man propped up in the hospital bed. "Where's the other half?"

"Your father should be the one to teach you," he said. "He should be here now."

Her father was serving three consecutive life terms at Seal Bay. She was never going to see him again, and she didn't want him teaching her any-

thing. She'd seen what he'd done. But this was no time to take her bitterness out on her grandfather. All she could do was wait for the old man to go on.

"*Someday you'll know what must be done. Someday your teacher will be found. Until then, be patient. Someday . . .*"

His last word had been *someday*. Sofia had waited a long time. Much of that time had not been pleasant. She'd stopped expecting explanations, or even wanting them. But now here she was.

Another vehicle pulled up behind hers at the end of the long drive. Sofia got out of her car at the same time a man exited the white SUV behind her. Tall and lean, he had very broad shoulders and lots of wavy brown hair. She was struck by the coiled energy and animal grace in the way he moved as he came toward her. She'd have to be dead not to stare, and she couldn't help but lick her lips.

Okay, the guy looked delicious, but that was no reason to be rude, or blatant. Sofia managed to get the spike of lust under control by the time he reached her, but felt awkward and embarrassed.

She turned her attention toward the Gothic pile of stone in front of them. "Do you think it comes with its own madwoman in the attic?" she asked. "Or do they have to rent one?"

"And do Heathcliff and Cathy have a guest-house out back?" he answered.

Wow, a guy who knew *Jane Eyre* from *Wuthering Heights*! His voice was deep and rich as cream, and she couldn't help but look at him and smile. She was immediately caught by the bluest eyes she'd ever seen.

She almost stuck her hand out and said, *My name's Sofia. Can I have your babies?* The odd, powerful reaction unnerved her, and all her usual mistrust and wariness rushed back. She immediately turned and walked toward the house. Who this guy was and what he was doing here didn't matter. She had her own fish to fry.

Jason waited a moment before following the dark-eyed Hispanic beauty, appreciating her long legs and the curve of her behind as she walked away. He also needed the time to recover from the psychic whirlwind that had hit him when they'd looked into each other's eyes. He'd gotten the impression that beneath the skin, she was a creature of fire. He also knew a caged animal when he saw one. He doubted this mortal knew the first thing about her psychic gifts, or knew that she'd unconsciously thrown up one of the strongest psychic shields he'd ever encountered.

He supposed he'd have to go inside to find out who she was and what she was doing here.

He joined her as she rang the doorbell. When no one came to the door after a couple of minutes, she muttered, "Now what?"

There was an ornate brass knocker in the shape of a gargoyle in the center of the heavy wooden door. Jason tried it. No one answered this summons, either.

He was prepared to force the door open, but the knob turned easily. "Shall we?" he asked.

"Isn't this breaking and entering?" the young woman asked.

"I have an invitation to be here," he answered. "Don't you?"

"Yeah," she agreed, not sounding at all happy about it. "All this mystery is *so* annoying."

He nodded and pushed open the door. The gentlemanly thing would have been to stand back and let the lady enter first. But a protective instinct kicked in, and he went into the house ahead of her.

The entrance hall was huge, and deeply in shadows, but the darkness didn't keep him from seeing the enormous werewolves waiting in the corners. Jason turned to slam the door on her, but the mortal had already followed him inside.

"What's the mat—" she began as the beasts charged forward.

"Get out!" he ordered, and put himself between her and the werewolves.

The beasts snarled and leapt, and Jason took them all on at once. Claws slashed him across the face and teeth sank into his calf, but he was the one left standing when it was done. It was then that he turned toward the door and saw the young woman staring at him. Her back was pressed against the door, her eyes huge with fear, and she was pale and trembling.

He took a step toward her, but turned as someone began to clap behind him. Jason didn't recognize this old man, but he looked at him in disgust. "Haven't I already passed this test?"

The old man smiled, though it was more of a sneer. "Who says the test was for you, vampire?"

Chapter Two

San Diego, Spring, Present Day

Sidonie Wolf took a sip of orange juice and looked across the restaurant terrace at the sun sparkling on the calm water. The fresh breeze that ruffled her short blond hair was scented with salt from the ocean and jasmine from the pots of flowers lining the edge of the terrace.

On the other side of the table, Tony Crowe was drinking tomato juice. His dark eyes held a twinkle that said he knew exactly how ironic the sight of a vampire drinking blood-colored liquid looked in this setting. "Hey, I like the flavor," he said when he put his glass down.

"Did I say a word, Daddy?" she asked.

Tony took a quick look around, but no one was sitting near enough to overhear. "Daddy?" He raised an eyebrow. "Sid, darling, what are you up to?"

To any mortal watching, they certainly wouldn't look like father and daughter, but that was what they were. Both looked to be in their twenties. He was dark, handsome in a sharp-boned, Central European, how-Dracula-should-have-looked-if-he'd-really-been-a-vampire way. She had the blue eyes and blond hair of her mother's side, but had inherited Tony's elegant cheekbones.

Sid smiled enigmatically and ate a few bites of omelet. Then she waved a finger at him. "Paranoia from the male parental unit? I'm hurt. How was the drive down from Los Angeles?"

"The drive was fine. Why are you calling me Daddy?"

They were Clan vampires, meaning that their culture was both matriarchal and matrilineal. Sid was a female of the Wolf Clan, the daughter of House Antonia. Tony was a Prime of the Corvus Clan, son of House Berenice. Technically, since Tony and Antonia were not a bonded pair, their child had no reason to call him "Daddy." But Sid was quite close to the Prime who had sired her and frequently referred to him in mortal terms.

"Okay, maybe *Daddy* is a bit much," she conceded. "How are you doing, Pop?"

He grimaced. "Let's just go with Dad, okay? I'm fine."

"Good." Sid sat back in her chair. She was finding this far harder than she'd thought it would be. "Are you still running security for the clinic? How's Dr. Casmerek? I suppose he's busy doing important research to help the diurnally challenged."

"I suppose he is," Tony answered. He looked very suspicious, but at least he wasn't trying any telepathic probing for her ulterior motives. "What are you up to, girl? Your daylight drugs don't need adjusting so soon, do they?"

She shook her head. "I was just wondering if he'd come up with any new wonder drugs lately. Or if he might be interested in other medical problems we have."

"He and his teams better be, with all the money the Clans and Families invest in their projects."

"Good. David Berus is in town, did you know that?"

"Is he?" Tony asked.

"Lady Juanita asked me to come to dinner tonight," she rushed on. "David Berus is going to be there."

The Clan Matri actually didn't ask, she commanded. Sidonie Wolf hated being ordered around. Even for something as ostensibly pleasant as being a guest at a dinner party for a respected Prime of the Snake Clan. Sidonie was not like other Clan daughters. At least she wasn't going to be if she could help it. Open rebellion was not an option, but guile . . . now, guile could work wonders.

As ever, Tony was quick on the uptake. "Lady J. wants you to mate with David. Congratulations. I look forward to being a grandfather soon."

"Oh, please!" she complained. "Not that I object to having a baby," she went on. "Or even several babies. I'll do my duty to the Clan. But I want the choices to be mine, without attachments and emotional complications."

"Then what's wrong with David? He's still heartsore from having lost his bondmate, so he's not likely to want emotional complications, either. Genetically—"

"He and I are first cousins," she pointed out. "His sire's Wolf Clan."

"I forgot that."

"The Clans need fresh blood."

He gave her a stern look. "Yeah, but the fresh blood you're interested in sprouts fur and a tail at least once a month."

"How's Rose?" she snapped back.

There was fire in his eyes when he answered. "She's eighty and just moved into a nursing home."

Sid hated herself for reacting so unkindly to his having touched a sore spot. "I'm sorry," she told her father. "But I think we just made the point that because of duty to the Clans, neither of us can have the ones we really want."

He looked thoughtful. "You have a plan. You always have a plan. You, my dearest, would make Machiavelli look like an amateur, and old Nick was one hell of a Family Prime."

"We females are always the smarter ones," she said, grinning.

Tony smiled back. "You want me to approach Dr. Casmerek about something, don't you?"

Sid decided she might as well be blunt and hope that the storm would pass quickly. "Artificial insemination. My egg, a donor's sperm—"

Tony shot to his feet. "Are you out of your mind?"

Everyone on the terrace was staring at them.

"Calm down." She gestured. "Sit down. Hear me ou—"

The cell phone in her purse rang before she could finish. Frustrated by the interruption, Sid flipped it open and demanded, "What?"

The answer from her partner at the Bleythin detective agency sent all her own problems right out the window.

"I'll be in as soon as I can, Joe," she said, and hung up. "Sorry, Dad," she told Tony. "We're going to have to have this argument later."

"What's the matter?" he asked.

"Cathy's gone missing. She's our office manager," she added.

"This sounds more serious than just calling a temp agency to cover the phones."

"Oh, yes." She nodded. "It's extremely serious when a werewolf who can't control the change goes missing so close to a full moon."

Chapter Three

The scrambling of sharp claws on hot concrete was louder in Sofia's ears than the sound of her own ragged breathing.

They were right behind her.

She could feel the heavy bulk of furred bodies close behind her.

They were faster than she was.

Why didn't they catch up with her?

Were they enjoying the chase?

Her heart pounded as she ran as fast as she could. Her feet slipped in the flimsy flip-flops, but they'd surely bring her down if she stopped to kick the shoes off. She dug her toes into the soft plastic and kept going. Traffic slid past on the street, people loitered on stoops and at storefronts as she ran by, but no one seemed to notice that she *was being chased by three enormous dogs. The sun hadn't quite set yet. Why didn't they see?*

She didn't have the breath to call for help.

She did cry out when one of the dogs moved up to nip her bare leg, and a warm trickle rolled down her calf.

The animals smelled the blood and began to howl.

She spotted an alley and remembered that there was a fence at the end of it that she could climb, and the dogs couldn't. One of her shoes slipped off when she made the skidding turn and she stepped on a shard of broken glass, but she kept running.

She was nearly at the end of the alley when she saw that she'd made a wrong turn. There was a wall where she'd thought there'd be a fence.

She slammed into the brick wall before she could stop herself, scraping her palms and jarring her arms from wrists to shoulders. She turned around and fell to her knees, putting her at eye-level with the dogs.

They had big heads, and huge teeth. Their eyes glowed, cruel and fierce, and full of hunger.

Their eyes glowed!

She grabbed a broken bottle from the ground.

They formed a half circle around her and stared at her for a while.

They wanted her to drop her weapon, but she wouldn't!

Then the largest one growled as if to say very well, *and all three of them began to move in for the kill.*

Northeast of San Diego, Spring, Present Day

"She's not with us," the old man said.

Jason put his hands on her shoulders and saw a nightmare in the woman's dark eyes. "You think?"

She was trembling and her heart was racing faster and faster. The woman needed help, but none of the mortals were going to step in to halt their stupid *tests*.

Jason tried gently shaking her, then calling to her, but he knew he'd have to go where she was— even though interfering with mortal thoughts was dangerous.

For him.

"You're having a panic attack. It'll be over in a minute," he reassured her.

But tears welled from her big brown eyes. What was a Prime to do? He pulled her closer and into a tight embrace. Then he kissed her.

Fire shot through him, and their minds joined

at the moment their lips touched. There was a moment of urgent passion, then . . .

The tangy scent of the blood of a terrified child assaulted his senses.

Anger overrode desire, and he was filled with an overwhelming sense of protectiveness. She was his! She needed help.

The shape of the world shifted, and Jason stood at the entrance of an alley. It was like looking down a long tunnel. At the end of it was a trio of beasts. Facing them was his Sofia on her knees.

He moved forward until he was in among the beasts. They turned claws and fangs on him, and he answered them in kind, keeping himself between them and the girl as he fought her attackers. After he turned them into bloody piles of fur at his feet, he turned and helped Sofia to stand.

When his hands touched her, she wasn't a little girl anymore and she came into his arms, warm and trembling.

And their lips touched . . .

Sofia was aware of the mouth pressed demandingly against hers and the sensual heat rushing through her, threatening to melt her bones. Her kiss was equally demanding; she wanted to taste all of him. His palm splayed across the small of her back, pulling them close, hip to hip. He was all hard muscle, and she melded to it. His other hand cupped the back of her head, possessive and protective at once. His thumb stroked down the back of her neck, sending a shiver through her. Her hands fiercely clasped his shoulders, never wanting to let go. He permeated her senses. He smelled male, and tasted male, and *felt* so male, it drove her mad with need. She had no idea how anything could feel so right so fast, yet their bodies fit perfectly together.

She'd never believed in perfection, and skepticism rose to pull her out of the nonsense of believing in this perfect kiss.

"What the hell are you doing?" she demanded as she pushed the man away.

She tasted copper and wiped the back of her hand across her sensitized lips. A drop of blood smeared across her hand and she stared at it. Hers or his? Hers, she thought, remembering that her tongue had touched one of his very sharp teeth. Some of her annoyance faded with the realization that she'd been as much involved in the kiss as he'd been.

His eyes twinkled. They were very blue. "You can't tell me you didn't enjoy it."

Oh, he was a cocky one. She had to fight not to be charmed by his insolence. "You started it. Why?"

He shrugged. "Seemed like a good idea."

Vague memories and nightmare images swirled around her. She had no interest in remembering the details. "I saw a dog. I hate dogs. I must've overreacted."

A flash of annoyance crossed his features, but all he said was, "Yes."

From his sudden coldness, Sofia sensed he was a dog lover. Well, that doomed any possible relationship. Which brought her back to . . .

"*Why* did you kiss me?"

"To calm you down."

"Aren't you supposed to slap someone when they get hysterical?"

"That's not my style." He cocked an eyebrow and crossed his arms.

A stern voice spoke from behind them. "Jason Cage, Sofia Hunyara, you have been summoned. It is time for you to learn why. Come."

Chapter Four

"Shall we, Sofia?" Jason asked, and took the mortal woman by the arm.

She resisted for a moment. He caught the thought, *What the hell am I doing here?* Then her curiosity got the better of her and she let him lead her forward.

"Do you know what this is about . . . Jason?" she asked as they followed the old man down a long, ill-lit hallway.

"Not really."

He could tell that she wanted his reassuring touch on her arm, yet feared any dependence; she fought the craving by deliberately stepping away from him. He shouldn't resent her lack of trust, but he did.

They were led to a large room lined with tall

bookshelves, most of them empty, and shown to a pair of threadbare wingback chairs. The old man sat behind an ornate but battered desk. Jason noted that much of the damage to the furniture looked like the marks of animal claws, and the wooden floor was marked with long, deep gouges. It looked like generations of wolf pups had run wild in the place.

"Show her," the old man told Jason.

"Show me what?" Sofia asked.

"Who are you?" Jason asked the mortal male.

The old man sighed and folded gnarled hands on top of the desk. "So much to explain—I don't know where to start."

Sofia glanced at her watch. "Talk fast."

The old man said, "Sofia, I am your great-uncle Pashta Hunyara."

Her expression went hard. "I don't have any uncles."

"Great-uncle," he repeated. "And there is a great deal about yourself you do not know."

Pashta? Jason smiled, remembering a fearless toddler in the Romany camp who used to climb onto his lap and demand stories. How quickly they aged.

"You know me, Prime," Pashta said. "Show the girl the one thing she can believe in."

Jason remembered what had drawn him to this

odd meeting and took the gold coin out of his pocket.

"Where did you get that?" Sofia demanded when he held up the heavy half circle of gold.

"It belonged to a friend of mine," he told her.

"It belonged to my grandfather," she said. She reached beneath her blouse and brought out the other half of the coin, hanging on a leather cord. "What are you doing with my talisman?"

Jason tilted his head toward Pashta. "He sent it to me, I think."

"I did," the old man said. "Are you going to snatch the other half away from the Prime and run away, Sofia? Or would you like me to explain everything to you?"

Sofia liked to think that six years in the navy had made her a logical, methodical, and disciplined person. Yet here she was, the wild child she'd fought to tame was trying to claw out into the open again at the first painful mention of family. She had to get herself under control—though being hit with equal parts lust, terror, and weirdness in the last few minutes was enough to rattle anyone.

She sat back down and made herself concentrate on the man who claimed to be her relative, instead of on the man holding the other half of her heart. It took all her willpower to remain polite. "Please explain."

Pashta smiled, and for a moment he looked just like her grandfather. "First, let me say that we have been searching for you for a long time. For you and your cousin Catherine. Where have you been all these years?"

Her suspicions heightened, and the mention of Cathy shook her. "*You're* the one offering explanations."

"What do you know of our family history?"

Sofia said nothing, waiting him out.

He sighed. "Our family is different. We have secrets, very deep secrets. We are blessed with great powers, and cursed as well."

Not to mention being full of bullshit, she thought.

Hear him out, Jason advised, his voice so clear it felt like he spoke inside her head.

Sofia turned sharply to look at Cage and was caught by his soothing, reassuring gaze.

This is hard stuff to explain. Harder to believe and accept. Give it a chance. Give Pashta a chance.

His calm voice caressed her soul; she couldn't be afraid with him beside her.

And *that* made no more sense than the old man's talk of curses and blessings.

"We are a tight-knit and insular people. We have to be. Your great-grandparents are the ones who made the decision to bring our people to America after the war. They wanted to start over, to escape the curse, to pretend that we are normal people."

"I *am* a normal person."

"You don't really believe that," Cage said.

She glared at him.

He smiled and pointed toward the old man. "He's beating around the bush because he doesn't know how to explain that a werewolf bit one of your ancestors, and your whole tribe has been hiding from the natural-born werefolk ever since. That about sums it up, doesn't it, Pashta?"

"Were . . . wolf?"

Pashta nodded.

She smiled. "This is where Marty Feldman shows up and says, 'There wolf,' right?"

Jason smiled at her reference to *Young Frankenstein,* but Pashta said, "What?"

"There are no such things as werewolves," she told the old man.

"Just because you've never been formally introduced to any doesn't mean they don't exist," Jason told her.

How did one get formally introduced to a werewolf? Shake paws?

That would be a polite way to start.

Jason sounded amused and calm, which helped her hold her temper. She didn't know why she found him reassuring when he might be as crazy as Pashta.

"What do you think those animals in the hallway were?" Pashta asked.

She didn't want to think about those slavering monsters. "Hounds of the Baskervilles," she said. "Go on about my family. Promises of information are how you got me into this nuthouse."

"We finally found you through the blog where you post about books and films on Live Journal." The old man chuckled. "It amazes me how anyone can be Googled these days. Some secrets are becoming too hard to keep, don't you agree, Prime?"

Jason nodded. "But we have to keep trying."

That's what she got for using her real name online. She sighed. "Go on, *Uncle* Pashta."

"Neither your father nor Catherine's mother wanted anything to do with our heritage, though they both had the gift. She wouldn't use it, and he . . . he misused it tragically."

Sofia made a sharp gesture. She didn't want to know anything about her good-for-nothing father, but she'd put up with hearing about him if she could learn other things. Her grandparents and great-grandparents had always been secretive and mysterious.

Maybe because they were hiding from nutty relatives who believed in werewolves.

"Once we finally tracked down you and your cousin, we asked you both here to explain your heritage to you. We asked Jason Cage to come because his skills are necessary to train you."

So where was Cathy? She glanced at Jason. "What skills?"

"I'm an animal trainer and stage magician," he said.

"You are the Beast Master!" Pashta proclaimed.

This sounded familiar. "Haven't I seen you on Leno?"

Cage gave a modest shrug.

"You work in Vegas, right?"

"Pay attention!" Pashta demanded. "This is important!"

"It's not our fault that you're making such a botch of the explanations, Pashta," Jason said.

The old man gestured at Sofia. "I've never had to explain this to a stranger before. We need her to lead the hunt, we need her to train the ferals, but she is not one of us!"

"Nor will she ever be, if you keep thinking

of her as an outsider. I can feel you reluctantly pulling out every word you say. It's giving me a headache."

"The truth is difficult."

Sofia seethed at knowing her relative wanted her only for some skill she supposedly possessed, even if he was a nutjob. Angry at herself for holding out hope again for some family connection, she got up. "That's it."

"Wait!" the old man called.

She heard his desperation, but walked out anyway.

Chapter Five

Jason rose, needing to go after her, and held up the coin. "What is really going on here?"

"Do you remember what happened during the war?"

"The experiments? Is that what you meant by 'It's started again'?"

Pashta nodded. "Some of our people have been taken. Perhaps they have Catherine, as well. She went missing soon after we found her. They may be looking for Sofia after today." He banged his fist on the scarred wood. "We need that girl. We need you to show her how to tame the beasts those bastards make." He gave a bitter laugh. "Though first we have to find the beasts, and rescue them."

Or destroy them, Jason thought, remembering back to 1943. "Who is doing this? Why?"

Pashta spread his hands out before him. "We don't know very much yet, but we have to act quickly. I'm trying to assemble a team, which is why I need Sofia and you." He gave him a hard look. "You will honor your vow, won't you?"

When he put it like that, Jason couldn't point out that American werefolk had their own system for dealing with problems. Besides, Pashta's people were not proper werefolk. They were as likely to be hunted as they were to be helped.

"I'll protect the girl," he said. "I'll train her."

Pashta pointed to the door. "Then go after her."

Because he could move faster than a mortal, Jason reached Sofia before she got into her car. He put his hand over hers as she began to open the door and said, "Let's start over, shall we?"

He was almost overwhelmed by the warmth and softness of her skin.

"You seemed like a sane person," she said as she turned to him. "I don't know why I thought that."

"It's probably because I'm so handsome and charming."

"Good Lord, I hope I'm not that shallow."

He ran his hand up her arm, delighted by the faint shiver this sent through her. "I notice that you aren't denying the attraction."

"The attraction isn't the problem. The fact that you're a nutjob who believes in werewolves is the problem." She glanced past his shoulder as an eerie sound filled the air. "Your SUV is howling."

He sent a soothing thought toward his wolves. "That's just George and Gracie," he told the suddenly tense woman. "You'll like them once you get to know them."

"You may have noticed that I don't do well around dogs."

"They aren't dogs. And neither were those creatures in the house."

She paled and swallowed hard. "Wolves, then."

Jason shook his head. "You don't *really* believe that."

"Of course I do!" Her denial was sharp, and genuine.

"You're a Hunyara. Some instinct in you knows the difference between dogs and wolves, natural-born werefolk and your own lycanthropic relatives."

She tried to back away from him. And who could blame her? He was going about this as poorly as Pashta. He wanted her badly and that was clouding his thinking.

"Let me tell you a story," he said, and lifted his hand to touch her temple.

Central Europe, Winter 1943

He went with the Romany to a small encampment far deeper in the forest. It was nearly dawn when they showed him into the shelter of a hut. Inside, a large group of people sat around a small fire. Smoke swirled around the low ceiling. The air was acrid, and hardly warmer than outdoors. Energy permeated the room, almost as visible to Jason as the smoke, and he was aware of being in the presence of several powerful mortal psychics.

Werewolves and psychics? He wondered what was going on, but waited for the others to speak.

One of the younger males bent forward and peered at him closely. "Are you as young as you look, Prime? What are you doing out on your own?"

Jason would have been offended had the questions come from one of his own kind. Now he only shrugged. "There's a war on."

The old man clipped the younger man behind the ear. "My son is rude, Prime. His name is Grigor. That little one skulking in the shadows when he should be in bed is my youngest, Pashta. I am Sacha Hunyara. And we"—he gestured around him—"are the Outcasts. People not of the mortal world, nor fully members of the super-

natural world. We live in hiding, we keep our secrets, but now we need help."

Being an outcast and fugitive himself, he was prone toward instant sympathy for them. But being softhearted toward mortals was what had gotten him in trouble in the first place.

"Explain," Jason said.

"What do you know of werewolves?" Grigor asked.

"That most werefolk are born with the ability to change shape to wolf, bear, or whatever they become at will, and keep sane while doing it. But a mortal bitten by one of the werefolk turns into a creature forced to shift into a maddened animal during the full moon."

"Precisely," Sacha replied. "Our people, Prime, are somewhere in between. The natural-born see the bitten as diseased, and a threat to their own existence. They are more likely to hunt down and murder the ones their own renegades are responsible for making, than they are to try to help them."

"Is there help?" Jason asked. "I'm sorry, but I don't know very much about shape-shifters."

"We tame them," Sacha told him. "The Hunyara took on that responsibility long ago."

"We had to," Grigor added. "It is better to tame than it is to kill members of our own family."

"Some of us carry the disease," Sacha said. *"An ancestor was bitten, and the tribe cared for him. He escaped during a full moon and bit his own wife and son. She became a werewolf. With the son it was different. Instead of turning him, the attack brought out the skill to reach into the werewolf's mind. Ever since then, some of our people become werewolves, and others are able to control them. I am the current Wolf Tamer of the tribe."*

Northeast of San Diego, Spring, Present Day

"Does that explanation work for you?"

Sofia heard the question as though it were asked from a very long distance, then she realized that Jason's hands were on her face, his body pinning her against her car.

The chill of winter faded, along with the firelight and the faces and words that filled her head. She blinked as the hot, bright afternoon came sharply back into focus.

"What happened?" She looked sharply at the man holding her. He was an illusionist, a stage magician. "How did you do that?"

"Never mind," he said, and took a step back. His hands moved to her shoulders, warming her more than the sunlight of the fading day. "I'm sorry that you're being asked to take a lot of things that sound like nonsense at face value."

The screwy thing was that, coming from him, she half wanted to believe this nonsense. Sofia shook her head. "One of us has got to be crazy. You, specifically," she added.

He laughed. "The supernatural is perfectly normal to me, but I understand your skepticism. Think about what I showed you." He glanced at the sky and sighed. "We'll talk later."

"What's wrong with talking right now?"

This was stupid! She should want nothing more than to run away from this guy, yet a knot of loneliness squeezed her heart at the prospect of him leaving. She was never going to see him again, was she?

"Don't look so sad." He stroked her cheek, cupped her chin in his palm, and looked deep into her eyes. She wanted him to kiss her again. "I want to kiss you, too. May I?"

He lifted her hand to his lips.

So I can find you again, his voice whispered in her mind.

She thought he was going to kiss the back of her hand, a romantic but terribly old-fashioned gesture. But she didn't mind because she'd been reading a lot of Jane Austen lately.

Instead, he bit her wrist.

Chapter Six

"How long do you think we'll have to stay?" Eden asked as they approached the Moroccan-style mansion Lady Juanita called home.

Sidonie Wolf knew that her sister-in-law wasn't comfortable around large numbers of vampires, and she certainly didn't blame her, considering Eden's family history. Normally she might tell Eden to just suck it up and live with the shame of being born into an ancient line of vampire hunters. It wasn't like anyone was going to bite her or anything. Tonight, however, Eden's attitude was tinted more with impatience than paranoia, and Sid was in complete agreement. She was even more anxious to get this duty over with than her mortal friend.

"Let's try to get in, smile at everybody, and get out."

"Roger that," Eden answered.

At least Eden carried her and Laurent's daughter, which assured her welcome. Sid hoped that little Toni would be the center of attention and darling of everyone's eye for the evening. Toni was going to grow up mortal, which meant that she wasn't going to help the vampire population problem, but she was an adorable toddler, all blond curls and pink cheeks and dimples. She got the dimples from her dad, Sid's brother, Laurent. Who didn't have to be here tonight because, after all, *he* was Prime.

"Putz," Sid muttered.

She deeply resented the fact that even at the dawn of the twenty-first century, thems with penises still got to have all the fun. She didn't blame Laurent, who was out on the streets searching for Cathy, but she seethed with fury at Lady Juanita for not allowing the female members of Bleythin Investigations to join the hunt.

"What?" Eden asked as they went up the wide steps leading to the carved double doors.

"Just pouting because I have to go in and be nice to everyone. Do you want to take a turn?"

"Yes, please," Eden said. "I could be hacking into the old laptop we found in Cathy's closet right now if not for this command performance. It's not that I don't love your Clan, but—"

"You don't."

"I love your mother."

"As well you shou—Hello, Matri," Sid said as Lady Juanita opened the door.

The Matri nodded regally. "Welcome, Wolf daughters. You will always have a place in my citadel."

Whether we want it or not, Sid thought, using many layers of mental shielding to keep her opinions to herself.

Besides, the Matri had spoken to them aloud instead of issuing a telepathic greeting. That set the ground rule for this evening. Sid understood why when another female appeared beside Juanita at the door.

"Hi, Mom," Sid greeted Lady Antonia, head of her house of the Wolf Clan.

Antonia had lost her ability to use telepathy, and it would be rude and cruel to use this sense when she couldn't. Besides, Eden didn't have a lick of psychic ability.

Antonia held out her arms, and Eden dutifully handed Antonia's namesake over to her grandmother. Then Lady Juanita ushered them into her home with an elegant, imperative gesture.

"I hear your sire was in town," Antonia said

as Sid walked beside her down the long entrance hall.

"He stopped by to pay his respects this morning before he returned to Los Angeles," Juanita said before Sid could answer.

She hoped he hadn't said anything about the conversation they'd had to the Matri, since he'd been livid about her suggestion of using modern medicine to assist their population problem. He had calmed down enough to say he'd talk to the people at the Los Angeles clinic, if and only *if* she could come up with a Prime who'd agree to the procedure.

She knew this was because he didn't think she had a snowball's chance in hell of finding a suitable candidate, since Clan Primes were so stupidly old-fashioned and macho.

And speaking of macho . . .

Sid was aware of the males waiting for them before they reached the garden courtyard. The energy that hit her senses was hot and spicy, filled with dark undertones of challenge and rivalry. The males of her own species always reminded her of cinnamon and pepper, black coffee and dark chocolate. They made her hungry. She couldn't stop the primal thrill of excitement that shivered through her.

But the call of male to female was normal

and natural, and Sid was able to acknowledge it without letting a rush of lust go to her head. She smiled at her sister-in-law when they reached the waiting males in the courtyard, and Eden grinned back.

"I might be bonding with my own gorgeous vampire," Eden whispered to her, "but I can enjoy the window shopping."

"It's too bad Laurent isn't here to defend his mating rights when the boys start hitting on you."

Eden's grin widened. "I'm not sure what's more fun: watching Laurent get jealous, or the way he stands back and smiles and lets me defend my own honor when the Clan boys gather. I'm not sure if that's because he accepts me as an equal, or because he's as lazy as he claims to be," she added.

"I think it's a bit of both," Antonia said. "Eden, come with me, there's someone I want you to meet. Sidonie, mingle."

"Aw, Mom," Sid complained at being left alone.

Eden gave her a sympathetic look, but dutifully accompanied the woman holding her baby.

"Motherhood makes us weak," Sid grumbled as she faced the crowd. Oh, well, it was best to get the social obligations over with so she could get back to hunting for their missing associate.

As she stepped onto the tiled courtyard, she glanced at the sky. Instead of seeing the beauty of the moon, she was gratefully aware that it was several nights away from being full. They had some time before Cathy was helplessly trapped in her lycanthropic form, but not much. They had to find her before then, because if she killed or bit a human as a werewolf, according to werefolk law she'd have to be executed.

To Sid this was brutally unfair. What was even worse was that the person who had to carry out the sentence was someone who cared for Cathy very much. Sid knew that if she lived the circumscribed life of a proper vampire female, this wouldn't be any of her business.

But she couldn't live like that, all cosseted and safe. It wasn't that the Clan women didn't have incredible power—personal, spiritual, sexual, financial—a Matri's word was law among her Clan, and only the Matri could override the decisions of the Mother of a House. But these powerful women weren't *involved* in the greater world outside their own domains.

Boring.

But this wasn't the time or place to proclaim her feelings. She took a deep breath, forced a smile, and walked through the crowd of males in the courtyard to stand next to the bubbling fountain in the center. There she turned and waited to be adored.

A pair of handsome Primes showed up before she finished moving.

"Mortals think they invented speed dating, but they're wrong," a richly amused male voice said behind her. "You boys move along," he went on. "The lady is here to meet me."

When the Primes smiled sheepishly and moved away, Sid knew the Prime behind her could be no one but the legendary David Berus.

Chapter Seven

The civilized rules of vampire society required that he be here, and Jason was scrupulous about obeying the rules since his youthful run-in with the law. He approached the mansion carrying a bottle of wine and two dozen bloodred roses, George and Gracie pacing at his side. He buried his own impatience and mentally soothed the wolves, even though he shared their restlessness. It was important to get the formalities over with, even if he was anxious to be somewhere else, with someone else.

As he expected, the door opened before he could ring the bell. He hadn't expected it to be opened by Lady Juanita herself, who wore the necklace of the Wolf Clan Matri.

She smiled, her eyes glinting in amusement. "Who might you be, night child?"

"A stranger in your territory, but a friend." Jason introduced himself, his family, and his house and bowed formally.

"I've heard of you," she answered.

"My bad reputation tends to precede me." He smiled and held out the wine and roses. "But I bring nice presents."

"Did I say I'd heard bad things?" She took his gifts and stepped back to let him enter. "You are welcome in my home." She glanced at George and Gracie. "The wolf may be our Clan's symbol, but some of my guests tonight are mortal and might find your companions disturbing. Will they be all right if you leave them in the library?"

"Perfectly all right," he replied smoothly. "I didn't mean to crash your party, Lady Juanita. I came to pay my respects."

"But you must stay. Let me introduce you to my guests."

What did one say to the most famous Prime of them all? Sid felt like an idiot, but all she could manage was, "Hi."

She had not planned on being impressed with David Berus, but some things simply couldn't be helped. He had an aura of sadness and hard-won wisdom that was instantly intriguing. Besides, he smiled at her in that appreciative, flirtatious way Primes had, yet she didn't sense any of the usual desperation that accompanied Primes meeting females. He didn't instantly want her simply because she was a girl. She couldn't help but like that.

"You are a perverse creature," he said.

"Tell me about it."

"Oh, I know all about you. Lady Juanita has been singing your praises since I arrived."

She had no intention of letting any other vampire know all about her, but she smiled as if she were flattered by the comment.

"Are you in search of rescue?" he asked when she glanced around.

"Not at all. I'm looking for—" She waved as her mother came into the courtyard. "Mom, over here."

She realized that she'd practically shouted while all other conversation among the hypersensitive guests was being conducted in murmurs and whispers. This brought stares and frowns, which were answered by a fierce smile from Berus.

"I only lost my telepathy, darling," Antonia said, coming up to her. "I'm not deaf."

It always amazed others that Antonia accepted a devastating disability with such matter-of-fact aplomb. But as she had once said to Sid, *"You can be alive or dead, and anything but dead can be dealt with."*

"Unless they're zombies," Sid had reminded her. *"But zombies aren't our problem."*

Werewolves weren't supposed to be, either, but Sid's worry for Cathy reasserted itself, and she was suddenly very anxious to leave.

Cover for me, please!

She sent the thought into her mother's mind, hating the necessity as she saw Antonia wince in pain.

But Antonia rallied, smiled at her, and came forward. "Hello, it's so good to see you again, David," she said, holding out her hands.

David Berus took them, and Sid moved away as Antonia imperiously demanded his complete attention.

Only to have another Wolf Clan Prime instantly step up to her. A second male put a hand heavily on the first male's shoulder. The first one's fangs came out. A scuffle began.

Sidonie sighed.

These meet-and-mate evenings were always the same; it was an ancient ritual overseen by the Matri and Mothers. Available females were trotted out for available Primes to vie for their favors in secure surroundings, away from any mortal eyes. A little blood might be shed for the sake of impressing the ladies and cooling the Primes' more violent urges. By the end of the evening, the females would choose one or two Primes as sexual partners. It was not unusual for the Matri to orchestrate which Primes the younger females mated with. Perhaps a child would be conceived, or the spark of a bond might ignite. Since there were far fewer females than there were Primes, it was always hoped that a female would produce several offspring with different fathers before she found a bondmate to settle down with. This was how it had always been done. For the continuation of the species, this was how it had to be.

Sid wasn't so sure.

Fifty years ago, vampires couldn't go out in the daylight. They couldn't tolerate garlic. The touch of silver brought agonizing pain. Modern medicine changed all that; why shouldn't it be used to change the culture, as well? What Sid needed was a volunteer to prove her point.

"I'll take him," she said as a stranger approached at Lady Juanita's side.

He had wavy brown hair and very blue eyes. You could probably seat six around the width of those shoulders. Long legs, trim waist. Assured, graceful walk. Beautiful hands.

Sid wouldn't mind having a kid with beautiful hands.

She smiled and stepped around the Primes fighting over her, even though the Matri gave her a disapproving look as she approached.

The tension level in the place went up when the blond woman smiled at him, and Jason would have preferred not to have the attention. Having a Clan female look favorably upon a Family Prime while surrounded by males of her own kind was not a good way for him to be welcomed into Wolf Clan territory. All he wanted was to get out of here and get back to Sofia.

Lady Juanita stopped and put herself between him and the other woman. She closed her eyes and touched his cheek, and the Matri's mind sliced through his shielding with gentle, determined skill. He could tell that he was the stronger telepath, but he suffered the intrusion politely. She was equally polite, taking only information important to the moment. And at this moment, Lady Juanita's mind was on matchmaking.

She was quite pleased when she said, "Blood sings in you, and calls."

He couldn't deny he'd tasted a mortal recently, but he wasn't so sure about that other stuff. "There is a woman who needs my help," he said.

"She's the reason I've entered your domain, Matri. I have a duty to her family that goes back several mortal generations, and I must fulfill my obligation." Clanfolk liked hearing about things like honor and duty and protecting mortals; their old-fashioned ethics came in handy for him.

"Does this mortal know what you are?"

"Not yet," he admitted.

"Does she know about us?"

"My obligation to her in no way compromises the secrecy and safety of your Clan. I ask permission to dwell in your territory for a time, and to hunt if I must. But I swear that my being here will bring no harm or attention to you and yours."

Jason spoke so that everyone within earshot could hear. He didn't want any of the Primes having even the faintest suspicion he was a threat. So he really wished the Wolf female would stop peering over the Matri's shoulder with a look like she wanted to eat him up. He wasn't in town to give the Primes competition in any form.

Lady Juanita studied him intently for a time herself, then finally nodded. "I thank you for seeking me out. I value your intention to honor your mortal debt. I grant the permission you ask for." She spared a moment to give a stern look to the other female, then added, "And I congratulate you

on finding the one every Prime is born to seek."
She dropped her formal attitude then and said,
"You arrived just in time for dinner. You will stay
for dinner, of course?"

She seemed genuinely welcoming, but Jason
wasn't tempted to spend the evening among his
own kind. "Sofia needs me," he said, though he
certainly hadn't meant to make any sort of desperate declaration about the situation. He was a
Prime who usually knew how to keep his business
to himself.

"And you need her as well." Lady Juanita's
smile was knowing.

Might as well let the Matri think whatever she
wanted. "With your permission?" he asked.

She gave a regal nod. "Go, for now. Know that
you are welcome in my citadel. Take my greetings
to your own Matri, Prime of Family Caeg."

"I will." He hurried out of the courtyard to
collect his wolves and get away before the female
he could feel still watching him put any moves
on him.

"Imagine that," Sid murmured as the Family
Prime made for the exit. "There's somebody here
who doesn't want me. Isn't that interesting?"
Since the last thing she wanted was to be wanted,
she followed him.

Only to be stopped by her sister-in-law as she reached the hallway that led to the entrance of the house. "Did you get a look at that guy?" Eden demanded.

"I'm trying to get a better look," Sid answered.

"Talk about melodramatic—he travels with a pair of wolves. I've never known any vampire to call attention to himself like that. Pretentious, no?"

Eden was descended from a long line of mortal vampire hunters. Before she'd become the bond-mate of a Clan Prime, she'd been more likely to sneer at vampire behavior than participate in it. She still had bouts of being terribly unimpressed with the culture of the ethnic group she'd married into.

Eden's news about Jason Cage set off alarm bells in Sid's head. "Wolves?" she asked. "Or werewolves?"

"I think I know the difference between wolves and werefolk by now," Eden answered a bit testily. "He called them George and Gracie—wait a minute. Do you think he knows something about Cathy's disappearance?"

"He said he was in town to help some mortal damsel in distress," Sid said. "No names were mentioned, but I don't believe in coincidences. I think we need to check this guy out."

It won't hurt to find out all I can about the sperm donor of my future child.

"Right now, we'd better get back to the party," Eden said, taking her by the arm and turning her toward the courtyard. "We've got at least an hour more of being dutiful Clan females before they'll let us skip out and get back to work."

Chapter Eight

The wolves snapped and poked their long, hard noses against her skin. They pushed her this way and that between them, playing an evil game. She knew it was a game by the way they grinned, showing huge, glistening fangs. She whimpered, blinded by tears. Deep down under the fear, she was furious for showing the weakness she knew they wanted from her. Sofia hated the animals as much as she feared them, but she hated the helplessness even more. Finally she got up the courage to beat against one's flank, but it took no notice of the blows. The fur was warm and soft, but she was more aware of the hard muscle underneath. These creatures could easily tear her to shreds.

Then a shadow materialized at the head of the alley, and Jason was there and . . .

* * *

Sofia shook her head and the drab motel room came back into focus. They were just dogs, she told her child's memory. Don't be so melodramatic.

And it had been her great-grandfather who appeared at the head of the alley, not some stranger she'd only met today.

The old man had saved her, and he'd died the same night. The exertion had killed him. She still blamed herself.

She didn't blame herself for what happened after that. Oh, no, only her crazy father was responsible for the next tragedy of that horrible day.

Stay, Jason ordered the wolves when he parked in the lot behind the small motel. *I know it's hard to teach a wolf tamer her trade without having the real thing to work with, but this has to be handled delicately. You want her to like you, don't you?*

He wanted Sofia to like them, even if that wasn't really necessary to the training. He wanted his wolf companions to accept the mortal woman as an alpha member of their pack, and the realization that he wanted these emotional commitments shook him. He was fulfilling an obligation with Sofia Hunyara, not looking for permanence, right?

He must be having some sort of weird reaction to the Matri's reading his mind. Maybe Lady Juanita had even put the notion of finding a mortal bondmate into his head to keep his attention away from the Clan female who'd been eyeing him. Whether it was obligation or sexual interest, he was anxious to see Sofia again.

He was all too aware of her presence calling out to him from inside a nearby ground-floor room. Heat raced through him, fueling the urge to be near her.

Gracie gave a jealous snarl and George glared when Jason got out of the SUV, but the wolves settled down as he left them.

He was nearly at the door when once more he found her memories flowing easily into him.

"Go to the hospital. Grigor needs you," Daddy said. *He continued loading the gun she hadn't known he had, while Grandpa stood in the middle of the living room, staring at him.*

They both stared at him, Grandpa's dark skin pale with worry, she barely aware of the aches of the cuts and bruises covering her face and body. She was so cold her teeth chattered. She didn't understand why she was freezing on such a hot day. Her muscles were tense with dread. The things she forced herself to focus on were crystal clear, but everything outside that small circle of reality was fuzzy and full of shadows.

"Why do you have a gun?" she asked.

"What are you going to do?" Grandpa asked.

"Protect my daughter."

Grandpa gestured at the weapon. "You know that isn't our way."

"Those bastards aren't our people. The old ways don't mean a damn thing to me. Go to the hospital," he ordered Grandpa. "Take Sofia with you."

She wasn't going anywhere with Grandpa. Her father was so intent on his own business, he didn't notice when she followed him out of the house.

He went to the motorcycle shop two blocks from their house. Even the local gangbangers had learned to steer clear of the bikers who'd recently started hanging out there. But her father showed no fear when he turned down the back alley and walked into the open garage in the back.

Shaking with dread, Sofia crept along the back of the building and peered cautiously inside the doorway just as the first shot filled the air with noise and the smell of sprayed blood.

She watched three men die, one after another. Then her father took out a knife—

"By the Goddess of the Moon, you are one messed-up woman."

Sofia heard the words, felt the warm strength of the arms surrounding her, and realized she'd been sobbing against Jason's shoulder long enough to get his shirt wet. "I'm not this bad normally," she answered between sniffles. "I've just had a rough day and—"

She pulled away from Jason. For a moment she was totally disoriented. Nothing looked right. The only thing that felt right was . . . him.

Then she realized they were seated on the bed in the room she'd rented for the night. Strangers, in a strange town, at the end of a very, very strange day. It seemed to have somehow gotten stranger still.

"How did you get in here?" she demanded. Somehow, she couldn't question how he'd found her. Having him with her was too disturbingly natural.

"I'm a professional magician. I always carry lock picks." This answer seemed too smooth and pat. She started to protest, but he added, "Can I buy you a cup of coffee?"

She didn't want coffee, but the walls of the room closed in on her like a prison. And the thought of a prison cell conjured up an image she never wanted to think about. Jason Cage's presence was reassuring, steadying, though she didn't understand why. The man claimed to believe in werewolves, for God's sake. And he'd broken into her room. Yet she trusted him.

If anyone was crazy here, it probably wasn't him.

She rose to her feet and held out her hand. "Let's get out of here."

He touched her fingers, and the contact was electric. Heat raced through her when he stood close to her.

"Lust is definitely clouding my judgment."

Had she really said that out loud? His smile was all the answer she needed.

"Let's save the coffee for later," he said, and kissed her.

She'd never needed anything as much as his mouth pressed against hers, devastating and demanding. The need that blazed in her burned away all doubts; sensation took her.

She clutched at him, ran a hand through his thick brown hair. *Such beautiful hair.*

His laughter flowed through her like champagne. *Shouldn't I be saying that to you?*

Your hair's prettier than mine.

His fingers tangled in her thick curls. *Eye of the beholder, darling.*

She wasn't so sure about this *darling* thing, but it sounded good coming from him.

Sound? What sound? Their lips were locked together and their tongues were busily twined around each other.

You're thinking too much. Don't.

The thought was commanding and cajoling at the same time. Then his clever fingers and lips worked magic on her skin.

It was only a step back to the bed, and they fell onto it in a frantic rush to pull off each other's clothes, eager for the touch of skin to skin. She'd never wanted anything as much as to touch and taste every solidly muscled inch of his body. She needed his claiming touch on every inch of her. Nothing had ever felt so right or real, and her body came to life like it never had before.

"I've never thirsted like this before." He spoke in a rough whisper, his lips brushing her ear. The heat of his breath sent shudders through her, as did the touch of his tongue gliding down her throat a moment later.

She suddenly felt sharp teeth pressing against tender skin and closed her eyes, waiting breathlessly. The urgency of his need pounded against her senses. This moment was important, imperative, though she didn't know why or how. Instinct urged her to flee or to submit, and submission was really the only choice. What would come next would be terrifying or wonderful, or both, but she didn't want to run.

You're braver than you think. Braver than I knew. Be mine.

Not a question but a demand.

She opened her eyes and stared into his, saw a soul as lost as her own, on fire with consuming hunger. Then she saw the sharp, bright fangs. Arousal ran through her, far stronger than the instant of fear.

She held on tight. "Yes."

Chapter Nine

Jason hadn't meant for this to happen, hadn't known he needed it to happen. Of course he'd intended to make love to Sofia from the first moment he saw her, but this . . .

I've found you at last.

He hadn't known he'd been searching for a bondmate, but here she was in his arms, his body covering hers, his mouth pressed against her warm, yielding flesh, her heartbeat matching his. Her need matching his.

It terrified him, but it seduced him even more. He couldn't pull back. He couldn't stop. She belonged to him.

And he took her, fangs sinking deep to draw the sweetest blood he'd ever tasted, heaven and honey and fire. Her life filled him, her soul sang in him.

Orgasms rushed through her as he took her blood and slammed through Jason with the force of lightning strikes. Soon his body was demanding more than the taste of her. He needed to be inside her.

He gave her one swift, fierce kiss, sharing the last drop of blood on his tongue with her. Then he knelt over her and she lifted her hips, urging the deep, hard thrust that took him into her. He gasped at the sweet, surrounding heat and moved in a slow building rhythm that brought them both to a long, shattering climax.

Jason rolled onto his back and flung an arm over his eyes.

Oh, Goddess, what have I done?

He had never been more satiated, or hungrier for more of the same. The woman slept beside him, curled against his side. He was all too aware of the pleasure and peace he had brought her.

It made him happy—and worried the hell out of him.

Had this been a normal sexual encounter with a normal mortal, he would be content with the mutual satisfaction they'd shared. The Families weren't out to protect mortals the way their Clan cousins were, but they did believe in fair exchange in all their mortal dealings.

If Lady Juanita was correct—and Matris always were in these matters—Sofia Hunyara was his fated bondmate. Not that he needed the Matri's opinion. He knew in his gut, in his groin, and most of all in his soul that Sofia was his destiny, his completion.

"Damn it all to hell," he complained to the ceiling. "Why now? Why her?"

She belonged to her own people. They needed her whether she knew it or wanted it. It was his duty to make her accept her gift, to train her and—

Let her go.

"You belong to me," he whispered, turning to her and kissing her on the cheek. "Always and forev—"

"What?" She sat up and groggily ran a hand across her face. A flash of fear went through her, and she stared at him for a moment as if she didn't recognize him. Then she said, "Oh, it's you." And yawned.

Jason had never felt more deflated in his life. Here he'd been making a declaration of his undying devotion and she—

"Oh, it's *you*," he repeated sarcastically. "We just had the best sex of our lives and you act as if—"

"How do you know it was the best sex of my life?"

"Believe me, I know."

"Arrogant, aren't you?" She pushed her heavy curls out of her face and grinned at him. "Arrogant with good reason. It *was* the best."

He gave her an acknowledging nod. No Prime could ever be accused of false modesty.

Sofia still didn't know what Jason Cage was doing in her motel room, but she supposed it made about as much sense as everything else that had happened today. Though she wasn't in the habit of going to bed with someone on such short acquaintance, getting all huffy after the fact would be hypocritical. She'd wanted him from the first instant she saw him.

And now she wanted him again. But the question was, now that she'd had him, what was she going to do with him?

Had he actually said something like 'You belong to me' when she'd woken up? If he had, what did he mean by it?

Something in her gut and the back of her brain told her she knew very well what he meant, and that she liked it, but she told it to shut up. She'd lost too many people already to expect any permanence in her life. Giving in to the faint hope of connection was what had begun this whole crazy day in the first place.

She got up and went into the bathroom. The first thing she noticed when she glanced in the mirror was the love bite on the side of her throat. She touched it, remembering the delicious pleasure that ran through her along with the slight pain when he bit her.

What an interesting man, and what interesting reactions she had to him. Interest like that could be dangerous—probably *was* dangerous. Maybe she should tell him to get dressed and get out.

Instead, when she came back into the bedroom she said, "Didn't you offer to buy me a cup of coffee?"

"Don't scream."

Sofia froze a step away from Jason's SUV. As his hand tightened on her arm, a stray breeze enhanced the shiver that went up her spine. She was alone in an empty parking lot with a stranger.

Oh, God, what had she gotten herself into!

What was he going to do to her? What did he . . . ?

"Don't show any weakness if you want them to respect you."

"What?"

"They always need to know who's the boss.

They'll keep testing you. It's the pack mentality."

"I have no idea what you're—"

Then she saw the malamutes in the backseat. "Oh."

They raised their huge heads to regard her.

"George and Gracie," Jason said. "Meet Sofia."

She looked back at the animals for a moment, then she glared at the man beside her.

"I do not panic at the mere sight of dogs," she informed him. "What kind of wuss do you take me for? Slavering beasts attacking me tend to put me on edge, but I'm perfectly capable of sharing the planet with man's best friend. Most of the time." She looked at the animals again. Their steady regard wasn't hostile, but it was disturbing. "Let's take my car," she suggested.

"Wuss."

She wasn't going to let this man think she was a coward. "Fine," she grumbled, and let him open the door for her. A cold nose touched the back of her neck as she fastened the seat belt, but she refused to flinch.

Cage noticed. "A point to the lady, Gracie," he said to the animal. "Oh, and they aren't malamutes," he added to Sofia as he put the car in gear. "They're Arctic wolves."

Chapter Ten

"You might have mentioned what those animals were before letting me into the car with them."

"Did they hurt you? No," he answered for her. "And you learned a valuable lesson about self-discipline."

She supposed he was referring to the fact that she hadn't jumped out of the SUV at the first stoplight and run away screaming. She had merely sat in frozen silence until he'd parked and escorted her into the coffee shop. Now, safely seated at a table with a large foamy latte cupped in her hands, she was finally able to voice her objections.

"Do you have a license for those things? Why would anybody want a pet wolf in the first place?

Shouldn't they be locked in a cage instead of—"

"They have a very comfortable traveling pen in the back of the truck," he answered. "But they'd rather be near me, where they can shed in the backseat."

She couldn't help but smile at this. She noticed a few silver hairs on the black jacket he wore over a white shirt. "And on you, too."

He nodded and dusted fingers across the front of his jacket. "Fur is my constant companion. The dry-cleaning bills alone sometimes make me question my choice of profession."

"What is the Beast Master doing in San Diego anyway? Shouldn't you be doing two shows a night in Vegas?" *Bare-chested and in skin-tight pants that show off your package?*

The heated look he gave her made her blush and worry that she'd spoken out loud. "I mean—"

"This started out as a vacation, became an obligation, and now . . ." He shrugged. "It's gotten very complicated—or maybe very simple. I'm not sure yet."

She wondered why she had this almost overwhelming urge to find out everything there was to know about this man. Everything she hadn't learned from looking him up on the Internet, that is. It was an odd compulsion for a loner like herself, but she'd been having odd compulsions since the moment she'd first laid eyes on him.

"If you were really a loner you wouldn't have come when your family called."

Anger shot through her. "They didn't call, they sent an e-mail. And stop reading my mind."

He just smiled. "I'm glad you finally noticed. You're taking it well," he added.

She banged a fist on the table. "You're being insufferable."

He bowed his head contritely before looking up at her through impossibly long lashes. "Smugness is one of my prime traits. I can't help it."

It was hard not to melt at the sight of those big blue eyes, but she tried her best. She sipped her latte and realized that she was very tired. She put the cup down as she fought off a yawn. "It's been a long day."

"And the strangest day of your life?"

Her gaze flashed back to his. "Not by a long shot."

He reached across the small table and took her hands in his. They were big, strong, capable hands, hands that had made love to her not long ago. She wanted them on her again soon, but right now she fought the urge to let his touch be comforting.

"Tell me about that day," he urged in a gentle whisper. "Tell me about you."

She was sure he could have made her tell him anything. Though it was insane, she truly believed he could invade her mind. She didn't know why his power excited her rather than frightened her.

Since he didn't take what he wanted, she decided to tell him. "Well, apparently I come from a family of insane people."

He shook a finger at her. "Facts first. We have a lot to correct about your opinions later."

She frowned but went on. "I'm an American mutt from east L.A. My mom died when I was little. This left me the spoiled only child, and female, in a run-down house with my father, grandfather, and great-grandfather. I guess the family came from someplace in central Europe. My father didn't let my grandfathers discuss it with me. I learned a few words of what I later found out to be a Romany dialect, but I've forgotten them."

"And you weren't curious about finding out more about your ancestry until recently?"

She shook her head. "Until recently I was concentrating on putting some kind of normal life together."

"Survival does tend to take up all of a person's attention when things get rough."

"You sound like you know all about what it's like when life goes down the toilet."

"Oh, I do. But we're concentrating on you right now."

His gaze caressed her, making her go hot all over. It was hard to go on with a sudden spike of lust zinging through her.

Sofia cleared her throat. "We didn't have much, we didn't do much, but it wasn't a bad childhood. I was loved and protected. Even when—"

This time she had to clear her throat because of the sudden welling of pain. She'd long ago stopped crying over the memories, but now her eyes blurred with tears. She ran the back of her hand angrily across her face.

"Then one day my grandfather came home with the news he'd been diagnosed with cancer. That same day, the dogs chased me. My great-grandfather chased them off, then had a heart attack and died."

"Your great-grandfather was Grigor Hunyara?"

"Yes."

"I knew him when he was young."

"*What?*"

"Go on," he urged.

The look in his eyes was too compelling for her not to. "My father—my stupid, idiot, hot-tempered bastard of a father—reacted to all this by going to the garage where the dogs' owners hung out and shooting three men in the head."

She'd watched her father then barbarically cut out his victims' hearts, but she wasn't about to add that gruesome detail to this already lurid tale, no matter how much she wanted to confide in Jason Cage. Some things couldn't be talked about. The pain of thinking about them was still almost unbearable after all these years. She could still see brain matter splattered against dirty gray walls. She could still smell the blood.

The nausea that always welled up in her when she let herself remember churned in her stomach. She tried to control it, but had to run to the bathroom to throw up like she always did.

Jason watched the bathroom door anxiously while Sofia was gone.

I will never again think I've had a hard life, he thought, miserable for her.

Why hadn't anyone told her the truth, he wondered angrily. Why hadn't Pashta told her about her father?

Jason knew why her father had killed those three men. At least, he was almost certain of the reason. Did he have the right to tell Sofia? She certainly wasn't ready to believe him yet.

It couldn't be easy to be mortal in this modern era. So many things that had once been sureties about the supernatural world had been taken away from them. Very few *believed* anymore, even fewer *knew*. His kind had helped push the changes to the mortal psyche, triggered by the scientific age. Scientific discovery had benefited everyone, vampires perhaps even more than mortals. Because of science, his kind could now live in the daylight, and because no one believed in them, they could hide in plain sight as long as they were careful and circumspect.

But it also made it very difficult to explain reality to those who had a need to know, he thought as Sofia returned from the washroom.

"Better?" he asked, and handed her a cup of mint tea he'd ordered while she was gone. "This will help."

She took a sip, breathed in the scented steam, and sighed. "Thank you."

He very nearly melted from her grateful look. Jason wanted to tell her then and there that he would do anything to comfort her, to protect her, to give her pleasure. She had him.

Why the hell did her people have to need her now, when all he wanted was her?

"What happened next?" he asked. "After your father—"

"He took a plea bargain and went to prison instead of getting a needle in the arm." Her dark gaze flashed fiery anger. "He got better than he deserved."

"Aren't you being a bit harsh on your own—"

"Why do you want to know, anyway?" Her fingers clamped tightly around the cup.

"Your family lost track of you. I was wondering how that happened."

"My father went to prison. My grandfather died two months after being diagnosed. I ended up in foster care."

"That had to have been unpleasant."

She smiled at his dry tone. "Understatement's a gift with you, isn't it? I got lucky eventually," she went on. "I eventually ended up living with a retired Navy SEAL and his family. I joined the navy when I finished high school, and spent the last six years mostly on sea duty and reading books. Now I'm a civilian, I'm going to college, and for no good reason I'm using my spring break to meet up with a bunch that claim to be relatives— and turn out to be crazier than my murdering old man." She folded her hands together on the tabletop. "How about you, Jason Cage? Where do you come from? What is there to know that I didn't find out about from your Beast Master website? How did you end up on the other side of this conversation? *Why* did you end up in this conversation?"

He pried her hands away from the cup and took them in his again. "At first I didn't want to be here. Now I can't imagine being anywhere else."

Chapter Eleven

Sofia snorted rudely. The fact that he sounded serious scared her to death. When he looked offended, she couldn't help but laugh. "I don't need romantic drivel," she told him, then ducked her head. "But that did sound—nice."

"I see," he said. "You tell yourself that you don't need what you want."

"I learned early that it's not wise to harbor expectations. And so far, this trip to meet the family has been a complete waste. Even my cousin Cathy isn't answering her phone or e-mail, so I probably won't get to see her while I'm in the area."

"Complete waste of time? How can you say that after meeting me?" He gave her a teasing smile. "You wound me. Ah, I've made you smile. I don't suppose suggesting your uncle Pashta would like to see you would do the same."

"You'd be right."

"I'm glad. This way I get to have you all to myself."

She wasn't sure what he meant by "this way," but the incident at the creepy house swirled around in confusing images in her head. "Let's not talk about it."

"All right," he said. "We don't have to talk about it."

He definitely meant something by that, but Sofia let it go. She couldn't stop the yawn that suddenly reminded her that it had been a hell of a long day. Let's see, travel, trauma, treachery, and great sex. Yep, she had every reason to be this tired.

"I have to go to bed. To sleep," she added at the sparkle in his bright blue eyes. When they rose to leave, she said, "I'll walk. It's only a block back to the motel."

"George and Gracie won't like being deprived of your company."

"I'm not interested in spoiling your pet wolves."

His arm came around her waist as they stepped outside. "That's a very good attitude. You always have to be the one in control. However, never make the mistake of thinking that a wild animal is your property."

This was doubtless good advice from a man who made his living sharing a stage with tigers, even if she wasn't ever going to need it. "Thanks. You're not planning on saying good night when we get to your truck, are you?"

"A gentleman always walks a lady home."

She couldn't bring herself to object, even though it scared her to feel so secure in his embrace. His warm touch fended off the cool evening air. Maybe it wasn't permanent, but being with him felt nice for now.

They stopped in front of her motel door. When he turned her toward him, she expected him to kiss her. Instead, he looked her in the eye and said, "There are things I have to tell you."

Annoyance shot through her. "I said I didn't want to talk—"

He touched her cheek. "We aren't going to talk."

"The Nazis treat the Romany the same way they treat the Jews. They send captured Rom to their death camps."

"I know," Jason answered Grigor. If he hadn't tried to help some Romany friends, he wouldn't be a fugitive from his own kind.

"They have scientists in those camps who conduct horrible experiments on the prisoners."

"So I've heard."

"One of these torturers discovered the Hunyara secret. They decided that a racially degenerate characteristic is responsible for turning us into beasts. They despise us, but they're eager to exploit us. Now the Nazis are hunting the Hunyara and taking them to a very secret camp. They're trying to make werewolves they can control and use. At first, they used other prisoners to find out how the curse is transmitted. They caged them with our werefolk during the moon madness. Now they have soldiers volunteering to be bitten." He laughed bitterly. "Can you imagine the damage an army of Aryan werewolves could do?"

Jason had no trouble imagining the bloody havoc it could cause. "This has to be stopped."

"We must rescue our people and the other Rom they've infected," Grigor agreed. "But there are too many newly made werewolves for me and my father to tame."

Much more than simply rescuing the werewolves needed to be done. The whole operation had to be obliterated—no evidence, no Nazi survivors. He needed to tell somebody in authority about these experiments, before all supernatural *beings were discovered and targeted. But he was a fugitive with no one he could turn to.*

It looked like he and a small band of Romany were going to have to save the world all by themselves.

"We did it before; now we have to do it again."

Sofia heard Jason's voice as though from a long distance away. What he said made no more sense than the minimovie that had been running in her head.

She blinked and found herself standing outside her motel room door. She could make out the parking lot past Jason's wide shoulders. There were streetlights, and a little traffic. She was in San Diego, not Nazi Europe.

She focused on Jason Cage. "How do you do that?" she demanded.

He kissed her on the forehead. "Think about what I just showed you. Think about it happening again, here and now. And that your missing cousin might be in danger."

"But—"

The next thing Sofia knew, she was inside her room with the door closed behind her. He was gone, she was alone—lonely and confused—and wondering which one of them was actually crazy.

Chapter Twelve

"Show me."

Smiling, Jason took her hands. "Just remember that you're the one who came to me in your sleep. I don't want you pissed off at me when you wake up."

Sofia wasn't sure where she was or how she'd gotten here, but she was certain that here was the right place to be. "I had to find you. My gut tells me—"

"Your awakening psychic ability tells you."

"—that this is all true. Cathy needs my help. I need your help. She's in danger, and it has something to do with werewolves."

"I do believe you are correct, my darling. What does your cousin know about werewolves?"

"Pashta said that he tried to get hold of both of

us to explain our heritage. She knows less about our Romany background than I do. We never discussed werewolves in our e-mails, but—"

The world twisted and changed before she could finish.

"Dreamscapes," she complained upon suddenly finding herself standing among a group of people in a fire-lit cave.

Jason stood in front of the group. He seemed younger. He was pale and thin to the point of gauntness, all cheekbones and shadows and burning blue eyes. The people around her were thin as well, their clothes threadbare and hopelessly old-fashioned. There was something familiar about each face she saw in the flickering light.

"Your people," Jason said. No one seemed to hear him but her.

She realized she was somewhere long ago, when her great-grandfather was that tall, grave man to her left, and her grandfather was the strikingly handsome teenager beside him.

"You're giving me a past I never knew I had," she said to Jason.

"Yes, but that's not why we're here."

"Why are we here?"

"To save the world from Nazi werewolves. Your attention, please," he said to all of them.

She'd been through basic training; she knew when to listen to a drill instructor.

"Somewhere deep inside every moonchanged creature there is a human mind. If you think you should feel compassion for them, then you are dead wrong. Or, I should say, you will be dead. Show anything but strength and dominance and you will rightfully end up with your throat ripped out."

"How can you know this?" the youthful version of her grandfather asked.

"Do you think my kind start out as sane and reasonable beings?" *Jason shook his head.* "Our males go mad when we come of age. We crave violence, blood, and females. We live to hunt. We seek out combat. We delight in fighting our brothers until the strong win and the weak die. Civilization has to be imposed on us with a will and hand of iron. The moonchanged are no different than our young." *He smiled.* "Except that they are easier to control."

One of her relatives snorted cynically and spoke up. "Teach your revered granny to suck blood, Prime."

"Right. You guys already know how to control crazy werewolves." *Jason turned his intense blue gaze on her.* "But you don't."

The world rippled and changed again; she and

Jason remained the only constant things in it. The link that bound them together circled around and through them. It filled her with bright hot sparks that pooled in her heart and her soul and set her insides ablaze.

"That feels—wonderful," she told him.

He held her close. "I know. But it's not helping."

"Depends on what you want to help." She traced her fingers up his back and through his hair. "You feel so good." Sofia touched her tongue to the base of his throat. "You taste good."

"Sweetheart, you have no idea how good I taste, but I promise sometime soon, you will. I want you," he told her. "All of you, body and soul—but right now it's your mind I need to pay attention to me."

"Isn't this attention enough?" She continued to kiss a line across his throat and felt the pulse racing beneath his skin.

He made a small, needy sound that triggered the strangest urge to sink her teeth into his neck. Animals growled behind her before she could give in to the impulse.

Sofia glanced back to see the snarling George and Gracie. "Shoo," she commanded them. "Who invited you into this dream?"

"I did."

"I'm not getting naked in front of your mutts," she informed him.

"It's nice to have your attention back on business."

Before she could ask him what he meant, the world changed again.

Damn it, I wish you'd stop doing that! *she thought.*

"Pay attention," he replied.

From that point on, the concept of words disappeared altogether.

"You do realize that you're in a lot of trouble, don't you?" Cathy Carter asked the younger of her captors.

She sneezed as she finished speaking, which lessened her statement's dramatic impact. She was having a terrible allergic reaction to whatever they were spraying on her and themselves.

The beefy teenager laughed, but she sensed his unease. He looked toward the locked door. "I'm not supposed to talk to you."

She'd been working on this one's fear from the moment she'd been kidnapped. "Then listen, and remember that this is not a threat. It's not long until the full moon. Come the change, you are going to get your throat ripped out."

He sneered. "Not by you."

She could feel the moon madness creeping closer to the surface. A taste for blood was starting to burn the back of her throat. She licked her lips and fought back the anticipation.

"Maybe it won't be me," she agreed with him. "But your pack is still going to die."

Handcuffs fastened her to a chair. The chair was inside a sturdy cage. The cage was in a warehouse that also contained trucks, vans, and motorcycles. She'd woken up in the cage after a trio of ferals snatched her outside her apartment building as she was leaving for work. Her captors had been coming and going all day, mostly ignoring her except for the kid they'd left to guard her. She didn't know how many of them there were, and it bothered her that they seemed to be getting ready to leave town.

She hoped the Bleythins showed up to save her soon, or that she figured a way out of here herself. Wherever the bad guys were going, she didn't want to go with them.

"When my pack—"

"You don't know anything about *your* pack!" the boy shouted. "We're your real family."

His reaction startled her. Surely the blond biker types she'd seen coming and going all day weren't the Romany relatives she and Sofia had been exchanging e-mails about? This bunch had a kind

of Aryan Nation vibe going for them. Several of
them sported shaved heads and swastika tattoos,
one of them on his forehead à la Charles Man-
son. Creepy.

"You're not my family," she said.

"You're a werewolf just like us," he snarled.

"That will do."

Cathy shifted her attention to the man who
had spoken. She hadn't seen him before, but she
knew a pack alpha when she saw one. Instinct
told her to avert her eyes and submit to his least
whim, but she wasn't about to give in to instinct.

"That's right," he said, stepping forward and
looking deep into her eyes. "The moon doesn't
control you yet."

Cathy was furious at the heat that shot through
her. "Who are you?" she demanded.

"Your destiny."

She made a gagging sound.

He laughed. "Call me Eric. I've been searching
for you for a long time."

"And why is that?"

"Because we are meant to be together, Catherine, my love. I'm the reason you are what you
are. It was because of me that you were turned."

Hatred seethed through her, along with complete disbelief. "The feral that turned me is dead."

Eric nodded. "He was a good friend and a

loyal follower. His sacrifice is greatly appreciated."

This was sick and weird, and sent a chill through her. "Sacrifice?"

Eric smiled at her gently, but the look in his eyes was possessive. "There's so much you have to learn about our kind. It's important to know that incest is taboo. We never mate with one that we have turned. I wanted you above all others, so a friend brought you into the pack."

Cathy's free hand flew to her throat, to the spot where she could still feel hot breath and sharp teeth sinking into her flesh. She remembered bright gold eyes, soft fur, and a heavy body pinning her down. She'd thought the wolf was going to kill her, but what had happened had been infinitely worse.

At least for a while.

Mike Bleythin had rescued her, from the terror and from the moon madness. He'd given her a pack, and protection. She still couldn't control the monthly transformation into a beast, but at least she no longer dreaded the change quite so much.

She focused every bit of hatred she could summon on the smiling Eric. "You *deliberately* forced me to become a werewolf?" He nodded. "You bastard."

He shrugged. "We should have been mated a long time ago, but the natural-born Tracker interfered with my plans for you. Now we only need one more thing before we can abandon this stinking mortal world and return to the wild, where we belong."

Cathy had no intention of running off to live in the woods like an animal. She had to find out all she could, think of a plan. "What thing do you need?" she asked.

"Your cousin Sofia, of course. Once she's turned as well, we'll have both of the Hunyara females bearing our offspring. You can't imagine the strength that will bring to the pack."

She didn't want to imagine it. She wanted to be sick. Even more than that, she wanted to rip out this smug asshole's throat.

Chapter Thirteen

$\mathcal{W}$ho would have guessed Cathy had a secret life?" Sid commented as she peered over Eden's shoulder at the computer screen. Eden had easily cracked the security on Cathy's laptop and now they were sitting at her kitchen table going through her e-mail.

"You're not referring to the secret life where she's a werewolf, are you?" Eden responded.

"That secret life isn't secret from us," Sid pointed out. "But we didn't know about Cathy's having a family."

"We all come from somewhere—with baggage," Eden said.

Sid nodded. "You speak truly, my sister. But Cathy has never talked about where she came from before Mike saved her from the feral that turned her. It's strange to find out that she's kept up with her relatives. I thought we were her family," Sid added a bit forlornly.

"Maybe you should think of Cathy as a little sister who hid her diary from you. We all need privacy, werefolk and vampires even more than mortals." Eden gave Sid a very discerning look. "We all have secrets. Some more dangerous than others."

Sid knew that Eden wasn't at all psychic, but she was far from stupid or unobservant, and all the vampires, werewolves, and mortals at the firm's office spent a lot of time interacting with one another.

"I have no secrets," she said as lightly as she could.

"Oh, no, a daughter of the Wolf Clan like yourself is too noble and forthright to ever scheme, lie, conspire, or connive to get exactly what you want, while denying yourself the one thing you don't think you can have."

"There are a lot of things I know I can't have. Vampire females have to tread very carefully and you know it."

"And yet, you are a career woman with all the perks of a Prime—in most things."

"In most things," Sid echoed hollowly. "And I shall continue to scheme, conspire, and connive to get what I want—for all the good it will do me in the long run."

Eden shook her head. "You don't have to be a prisoner of your gender."

"For the sake of the continuation of the species, and the honor of my Clan, in the end, I will be. I'm just trying to put off the inevitable as long as I can."

"And you'd never openly rebel?"

"You know I won't."

"You Clan folk are such hopeless, selfless romantics. Not that I'm complaining," Eden went on before Sid could argue. "If you hadn't decided to go searching for your long-lost brother, neither he nor I would have ended up as part of the Bleythin-Wolf menagerie. He was terrible at being a villain and I made a lousy vampire hunter, so Laurent and I have a lot to thank you for. You and Joe, and Mike and Harry and Marj and Daniel, and Cathy, our lost feral sister."

Sid noticed the slight emphasis Eden put on Joe Bleythin's name, and her heart pricked just a little with knowing that here was one more person who shared the knowledge Sid could never share with him.

"Let's concentrate on Cathy." She firmly called their attention back to the far more important subject. "Read on."

Eden opened up another saved message in the Sofia file, but Daniel Corbett came into the kitchen before Sid could read the e-mail.

"See anything?" Sid and Eden both asked.

He blinked from behind his glasses and ran a hand through unkempt blond hair. They'd left him sitting in Cathy's bedroom doing his psychic thing while they searched the computer.

"I doubt it," Daniel answered. "I'm not sure if what I caught was glimpses of the past, or scenes from a horror movie set in World War II." He scratched his jaw, where faint stubble of a beard showed how long he'd been up. "Somehow I don't think Cathy's disappearance has anything to do with rescuing gypsy werewolves from evil Nazi scientists."

Sid looked at her retro-psychic mortal cousin in disbelief. "What did you eat before going into your trance?"

"My gift's obviously no use this time," he said. "I think I'll see if Joe and Mike need help. Has Laurent picked up any news from his sources?"

It sometimes came in handy that Laurent Wolf had not always walked on the good-guy side of vampirekind. He knew a lot of dubious characters out on the streets who wouldn't talk to anyone else at the Bleythin agency.

Sid tapped a finger on her forehead and held up a cell phone. "Not a word so far."

Eden sighed, in the way of a female missing her bondmate. "I really hate not going along for backup when he's dealing with scum."

"I'm sure he wishes you were there, too," Sid said.

Laurent was probably the only living Prime who didn't object to having a mortal female as a fighting partner. Eden and her brother were definitely the black sheep of the Wolf Clan.

"Try checking for temporal connections at the office again," Sid suggested to Daniel. "You might have more luck without the rest of us around contributing psychic white noise."

He nodded and left. This time her cell phone rang before she could read the e-mail. It was Joe.

"Still not a trace of a scent," he reported.

"Could a vampire be involved?" Sid asked her werewolf partner. "You know how we can mess up your sensing."

"What would a vampire want with a werewolf?"

What indeed? "I have no idea. But there was a Family Prime at Lady Juanita's tonight. I've got a feeling he's involved in this somehow."

"But what *is* this?"

"I don't know. But my senses tell me that there's somebody out there who wants Cathy for a really evil reason."

Joe growled. "You think it's this vampire?"

"I think he's involved, but I don't know why. Not yet."

"It's best to let vampires handle vampires," Joe said. "Mike and I will keep looking for the were-wolf connection."

Eden gave Sid a skeptical look when she put the phone down. "I was under the impression you liked this Cage guy."

"I like his genetic potential," Sid answered. "That's not the same thing."

Finally, as dawn neared, she started reading Cathy's e-mail correspondence.

Chapter Fourteen

$\mathcal{T}$o save the world from Nazi werewolves," Sofia murmured as she woke up from the long and complicated dream.

How did the subconscious come up with stuff like that? She chuckled and stretched out along the comfortably warm length of the man in the bed beside her.

The man in the bed beside her?

Wait a minute.

Her head rested on a bare shoulder, and an equally bare arm was wrapped protectively around her. When she opened her eyes she saw Jason Cage, and for a moment joy flooded through her.

Then she recalled that she'd gone to bed alone and sat bolt upright. "What the hell are you doing here?"

He opened one eye and grumbled, "Trying to sleep."

She didn't remember him arriving in her room. She knew she hadn't answered a knock on the door and let him in. Yet, she had the impression of having welcomed him into her . . .

Into her what?

Sofia rubbed her temples. Her mind felt stretched, and different. There was a lot of jumbled-up information swimming around in there and—

"You'll have a migraine if you try to make your conscious mind straighten it all out."

"Confusion seems to be turning into the normal state of things, and I don't like it," she told him.

"I don't blame you. But let it go. Relax." His deep voice was oh so soothing.

He sat up and began to knead her tense shoulders with his strong fingers. She couldn't help but close her eyes and lean back into the pressure.

"What am I going to do with you?" she asked. "I didn't ask you to be here. I don't know how you got here. I—"

"Don't want me to be anywhere else," he finished for her.

His hands moved down to cup her breasts and her nipples went instantly hard against his palms.

As desire pulsed through her, Sofia knew she couldn't argue with what he'd said.

Making love made more sense than the sorts of conversations they had, anyway.

She turned in his arms and drew his mouth down to hers. Her tongue explored and grazed across sharp canines. For a moment she tasted the metallic tang of her own blood, bringing her to the brink of orgasm. Then his hands on her took her over the edge.

He'd known he couldn't keep from making love to Sofia again, but he'd sworn that he'd keep from tasting her. That promise flew right out the window when he accidentally drew blood merely with a kiss. Her pleasure resonated through him. He'd never known a sharing of desire and fulfillment to match this. He needed more. To give her more, to take more.

I want you in every way. Want me. Need me.

Only you, was her answer.

He tasted her all over then, a drop from each soft breast, from her warm, pulsing throat and each wrist, her belly and the inside of each thigh. His tongue worked magic, soothing and caressing each place where he marked her as his. She panted and writhed as orgasms burned through her blood, and he tasted them on his tongue.

* * *

What was the man doing to her? How could anything feel so good? She clutched at him and clawed and begged for more, though she didn't know how there could possibly *be* more sensation.

Then he came inside her and she rose to meet every hard, fast thrust. Orgasms rippled through her, but—

More!

In response to desperate need, she lifted her head and bit down hard on his shoulder until the taste of molten pleasure filled her.

Jason shouted as her teeth sank into his skin. His body stiffened, and as he came, Sofia went with him, the explosive force of pleasure taking them down into the dark together.

"You bit me," he accused, and moaned. "I really wish you hadn't bitten me."

Sofia became slowly aware of the voice that whispered in her ear and slowly processed what Jason had said. It took her a bit longer to assess her surroundings. Their arms and legs were all tangled together. Pleasant aches and aftershocks pulsed through her. She was sticky with sweat, and thoroughly happy.

She didn't remember many of the details of

what they'd done, but that one, she did recall.

"You bit me first," she defended herself.

"It's all right for me to—"

"You *bit* me!" She untangled herself from his embrace and sprang out of bed. She clapped a hand over a spot on her bare breast.

He sat up on his elbows and stared at her. "Yes?"

"You said that people became werewolves by being bit. Am I going to turn into a werewolf?"

"I'm not a werewolf."

Relief flooded her for a moment.

Then he added, "I can't even turn you into a vampire. It doesn't work that way."

She stared at him in shocked disbelief for a moment, then she threw back her head and laughed. "Oh, you had me going for a minute. I'd almost started to believe this werewolf stuff." She looked at him and sternly shook a finger. "Let's not add vampires to your weird tales, okay?"

His expression turned guarded, and it took him a while to answer. "Okay."

She became aware that a sexy naked man was in her bed, he was staring at her, and that she was just as naked as he was. How did this keep happening? It had to stop. Okay, he was great in bed, but the guy was crazy, and increasingly making her think she was. If she wanted to deal with crazy people, she could return to her relatives' desert lair.

She glanced at the clock on the bedside table, then edged toward the bathroom. "I would like you to leave now."

He touched his shoulder, drawing her gaze to beautiful, bare skin. "You bit me."

"I'm sorry."

"I'm not."

There was something very important going on here, important for *them*, but she wouldn't let curiosity get in the way of her sanity. There was no *them*.

"Please leave, Jason. There's somewhere I have to be. Something I need to do."

"You're going to go looking for Cathy. You need my help."

He was wrong about her needing him. She couldn't afford to let herself need anyone.

"Please leave," she repeated, and walked into the bathroom, locking the door behind her.

Chapter Fifteen

Jason stood up and stretched and considered where to go from here. His lady had asked him to leave. Honoring her wishes would be the chivalrous thing to do.

"Screw that," he muttered.

He heard the shower go on, and within moments her scent came to him on a warm current of air. He got up and went into the bathroom.

She spun around when he joined her in the shower, and he had to grab her around the waist to keep her from falling. Her eyes went wide and she opened her mouth, but he didn't give her time to speak.

"Meeting one's bondmate is supposed to be a joyous but fairly simple stage of life. It's supposed to go down like this: True lovers look into each other's eyes, recognize kindred souls, share blood and sex, and settle down to live happily ever after," Jason informed the woman who had been born to be his.

"Say what?"

"The Prime involved shouldn't have to have obligations to the female's family that could keep her from him, but that's how our story goes."

"Our story?"

He cupped her wet face in his hands. He wanted to kiss her, but he had too much to get off his chest first. "The female half of the bond shouldn't be so prickly and terrified of trusting anyone."

"Are you talking about me?"

"I'm talking about us."

"There isn't any—"

"Let me finish. When you bond with a Prime, you're supposed to instinctively recognize your true love—that would be me. I recognize you. And I think you recognize me."

"But—"

"There sure as hell aren't supposed to be werewolves involved."

"You're a nutjob," she told him. "Please get out of this shower."

Despite her words, he knew she wanted to believe him.

Her instincts just need a little kick-starting. Or maybe she and I need to concentrate on us, instead of her family's problems.

Except that her family's problems could easily turn into deep, dark problems for the supernatural world, and the wider mortal world as well. If there was a pack of feral werewolves out there, bodies were going to start turning up in growing numbers. It was going to take as many wolf tamers as they could find. Which meant he had to train Sofia as quickly as possible without letting romance get in the way.

"I shouldn't be talking like this," he said.

"Like a crazy person?"

"You didn't think I was crazy last night. And I'm not talking about the sex," he assured her. "Those weren't dreams. I was teaching you, sharing knowledge."

A spike of fear ran through her. "You really were in my head?" Anger followed the fear. "How dare you?"

"Because you and I cannot let it happen again."

"Let *what* happen again?" Her shout rose above the rushing water in the shower.

Jason reached around her to turn off the faucet. When she tried to dodge past him he picked her up and carried her back to the bed, even though they were both soaking wet. He held her close while she struggled futilely. When she started to scream, he stopped it with a kiss. She both responded and rebelled, her lips clinging to his while she still tried to strike at him. He rolled her onto her back and held her down until she stopped struggling, at least physically.

The only excuse he could give himself for his behavior was that she had asked for his help and she was going to get it, no matter how much she fought against it.

It's so much easier to deal with tigers than stubborn mortals.

Her mental reply was so profane that he threatened to wash her brain out with soap. The woman swore like a sailor.

I was a sailor.

For some reason this struck her as funny, and her amusement rippled through her and into him. The feeling was almost as delicious as lust, but he forced himself to ignore the urge to explore this connection any deeper. He already knew she was the right mate for him. Why delve deeper into the bond now when any hope of having a future together might be futile?

Do you want to help your cousin? he asked.

You know I told you I do. I remember now, what happened in our dream. You taught me something dark.

How to harness the dark.

How did you—?

Lesson time again, Jason interrupted. *Watch. Learn. Come play with me if you can.*

Sofia knew a challenge when she heard one.

I don't play games, she told him.

No?

She knew he was aware of the eagerness coursing through her that gave the lie to her words. It amused him, but not as much as it surprised her. She had never been interested in competition before encountering Jason. What was this man bringing out in her?

Are life and death stakes enough for you? he asked.

Are there any other kind? she replied.

Then come with me.

It was dark here in the forest, and cold. She looked up at a sky full of stars, and the huge full moon terrified her. She reached out and Jason's hand closed comfortingly around hers.

"This is not a good idea," she said.

"I agree," he answered.

"Then why go tonight," Grigor asked, "when they're all moonchanged?"

"None of us are werefolk," Jason explained.

"It's easier for us to recognize them in wolf form."

"It's going to be bloody," Grigor complained.

Jason's eyes lit with anticipation and he gave a dangerous grin. His voice was a silky purr. "Oh, yes."

Sofia had never been so turned on in her life.

They stood in woods at the top of a hill. The camp was in the center of the valley below. Wolves howled inside the fenced compound and stalked along the fence line. Soldiers stood at the gate and inside the watchtowers on the four corners of the site. The cleared ground surrounding the place was brightly lit by the moon. Anyone approaching would be an easy target.

"The beasts know we're here," Grigor said. "But they can't tell the Germans."

"The racket the wolves are making tells them something's up," Sofia said. "I wonder if they're going to let the monsters loose to hunt us?"

"That would be fun," Jason said. "For us, not the beasts," he added when she gave him a skeptical look. "But the Germans won't risk letting their prize experimental weapons loose on the world until they're sure they can control them."

"Those experimental weapons are people!" Sofia complained.

"Most of the time," Grigor said.

"Let's go get them and see what we can do with them," Jason said. "Wait here while I take out the guards."

He gave her a swift kiss, then he was gone.

Despite the bright light, all she could make out was a blur of movement. Then she saw men go down and she knew they wouldn't be getting up again. Sofia's heart twisted at knowing Jason was a killer, but necessity kept her from dwelling on it.

A muffled scream came from one of the guard towers. Jason appeared at the tower opening as the sound died, and waved. She imagined that the shadows around his mouth were blood.

"Let's go," Grigor said.

He loped down the hillside, and she followed.

Deadly danger lurked inside, but Sofia didn't hesitate. She kept repeating to herself that the beasts were people and they needed her help. Knowing this helped fight off the fear.

Until she saw the huge furred bodies, the snarling muzzles, and glowing eyes of the creatures she'd come to save. They surrounded her, trapping her between the fence and the wall of a building.

They didn't want to be saved. They wanted to feed.

"Oh, crap."

You know how to do this, *she told herself as she was backed against a rough wooden wall. She saw the malevolence in their eyes. Hot breath steamed in the air; the stench of it blew across her skin and burned in her nostrils.*

She wanted to scream, but knowing the beasts relished her fear kept her quiet.

Take power over them, *she remembered Jason telling her.* You have to be in control. Look them in the eye until you make them yield.

Since she couldn't flee, she had to fight. The beasts were mindless killing machines armed with fangs and claws and thick, heavy muscles. All she had was her mind, which Jason assured her was enough.

Believe in me, *his voice whispered from far away.* Believe in yourself.

With no other choice, and no other armor, Sofia glared around the circle of approaching monsters. Her heart hammered in her chest and her knees threatened to buckle, but she couldn't let any fear show. These creatures accepted only strength. She had to be stronger than they were, in her heart and in her soul.

She put all of her will into looking at the beasts, not just at them but into them. Madness batted at her senses, wildness as sharp as claws ripped at her sanity. She knew their lust to taste her flesh and blood and threw it back at them, shaped into defiance and scorn. Who were they to think they could kill her?

"I am alpha here!"

She said it aloud, and into the werewolves' perceptions as well.

One of the werewolves lay down and rolled onto its back. A second one sat on its haunches. But a third one, the largest and fiercest, growled and took a menacing step forward. Another rushed from the side to nip at her leg.

The pair of them distracted her enough to break the hold she had on the others.

When they rushed toward her as a pack, panic took over and all she could do was scream.

Chapter Sixteen

It's all right. It's all right, sweetheart. You know I would never let anything hurt you."

"You were going to let them kill me!"

Jason held Sofia close and rocked her while she sobbed. She clung to him so tightly her nails bit into his shoulders, even though vampire skin was tougher than mortals'. He didn't mind the pain. He did mind her accusation.

"You have to do this on your own," he told her. "You have to have confidence in your abilities. You were doing fine."

"They were going to kill me! They always try to kill me!"

"You are getting the hang of how to control the beasts. You have to believe that you can save yourself."

She lifted her face to look at him, and the look in her eyes tore his heart, touching every primal, protective fiber of his being. The connection and desire that rushed through them when their lips met could not be denied.

He soothed her with kisses, and long, lingering caresses. Her fingers moved over him frantically, bringing fire wherever they touched.

"I want to build it slowly for you, let pleasure wipe away the fear," he told her, kissing her navel and then moving down to her clit. It was already swollen and moist.

She gasped and arched against his mouth. "No!" Her hips lifted insistently. "Now!"

Possessive delight went through Jason, heightening desire into a storm. "Happy to oblige your every wish, my lady."

Everything came down to the need to make love to her. Everything came down to becoming one with her.

He moved onto his knees and she guided him inside. He took a moment's pleasure at being sheathed within her soft heat before settling into hard, swift strokes. Her cries of pleasure drove him into a wild frenzy.

Sensation, pure explosive waves of it—it was all she wanted or needed for the longest time.

Sofia didn't know how long it was before she fell back into the real world, if indeed that was where she actually was when she finally opened her eyes. She saw a plain white ceiling above her, felt the bedding beneath her. Jason Cage was lying on top of her, and nothing had ever felt so right or natural against her skin as he did.

Amazing.

Fantastic, was his reply.

This time she didn't doubt for a second that he spoke inside her head. He began to stroke her breasts and tease her nipples, which distracted her for a while.

Is all we think about sex? she finally asked, not bothering to speak aloud either.

At least you included us both in the question.

But there are other things. Important things. We're being selfish.

We're bonding. The instinct tries to drive out everything else.

Well, tell it to stop.

Why do you think it's called an instinct?

We should be able to control it.

The way you're able to control werewolves?

Not fair!

She pushed his shoulder and he rolled onto his back. Sofia sat up, bunching the sheet around her, and looked down at the glorious man in her bed. It was *her* bed.

"I distinctly remember asking you to leave." It seemed like hours ago. She glanced at the bedside clock. It had only been a few minutes. "Didn't we just make long, lingering passionate love?"

With a smug smile, Jason propped his hands behind his head. "It's all subjective, isn't it?"

Sofia thought back over everything she'd experienced—in the last few minutes. "It really happened, didn't it? My great-grandfather was there, only no older than I am, and you, and me." She ran a hand over her suddenly aching forehead. "I was with you when you raided the German prison camp."

He reached out and took her hand. He kissed her palm, then answered, "Yes. The rescue mission really happened, and Grigor and I were successful, though that was only the beginning. This time I brought you along as a training exercise, and to show you what we might be up against again."

She was beginning to believe him, despite how crazy it all sounded. It was other aspects of their telepathic sharing that disturbed her. "It actually happened—sixty years ago."

"Over sixty."

"How old are you?"

"Obviously over sixty." He flashed a bright white smile at her. "Well preserved, aren't I?"

She wasn't susceptible to his snarky charm at the moment. In fact, she found him irritating, and disturbing. "You killed a lot of people that night."

He sat up and turned serious. "There was a war on, Sofia. You have a military background; you should understand the necessities of war."

Maybe she should, but she never had. "I joined the navy to pay for my education. I served on an aircraft carrier, but nowhere near the flight deck where all the testosterone flowed. I don't understand killing."

He touched her cheek. "Yes, you do."

She jerked away. "You enjoyed killing. I could feel it."

He looked at her intently, his gaze boring into her soul. "What did you feel?"

She closed her eyes and the sensations all came back. "Darkness running through you like a rushing river threatening to flood. Blood—not bloodlust, but . . . a craving, a craving for human blood."

"That is part of my nature."

"I don't understand. You said you're not a werewolf. What are—"

"What I was at the time was arrogant but

idealistic. The craving was also stronger then; I wasn't as much in control." Jason shrugged. "I was very young during that war."

She could accept that Jason had psychic powers, but she couldn't deal with the fact that he liked killing people. She knew she should fear him, but even knowing what she knew about him, her attraction to him was as strong as ever. What kind of sick fool was she? Just how badly had watching her father murder three men warped her?

"About your father," he said suddenly.

"Stop reading my mind!"

"I can't really help it," he answered. "I'm not influencing your thoughts," he added hastily, "but I am using telepathy to teach you."

"I know that," she snapped back.

He smiled at her annoyance. "You trust me."

It was probably stupid of her, but for some reason she did. "I don't think you'd abuse your power."

"Not now," he said. "Not ever again, but I have to tell you that I did once. And I was deservedly punished for it. That's why I want to talk about your father—because I understand his situation."

"You don't understand *anything* about my father."

"I know it hurts you to think about him. I don't want to hurt you, but—"

"Then shut up about it."

"You mean about *him*. You don't know how lonely his life is, how hopeless. But I've been in prison; I do know what—"

"Damn it, you're a criminal, too?"

She most definitely did not need a man like this in her life. There was nothing a violent ex-con could teach her. Nothing she wanted from him.

Except sex. God, what the man did to her in bed!

But she could and would live without it. The important thing was finding her cousin, making sure Cathy was safe. She certainly wasn't going to introduce a psychic psychotic werewolf hunter to her nice cousin Cathy.

"Get out," she said. "I mean it this time."

"You meant it the last time," he reminded her. He didn't look like he was going to budge.

She sneered. "What about all that 'happy to oblige your every wish'? Or does that only apply to sex?"

He looked very much like he wanted to argue with her. Anger crackled from him, and for a moment she felt vulnerable and scared.

Then he sighed and got out of bed. "All right, I'll go."

Once he said it, every fiber of her being ached for him to stay. The thought of losing him devastated her, but Sofia fought off this crazy reaction and bit her tongue. She turned her back on him as he dressed. She stared at the wall until she heard the motel room door close behind him. She wanted to run after him and beg him to come back, but she reminded herself that it was better for her to be alone.

Once she got herself under control, she picked up her cell phone and tried dialing Cathy's cell phone one more time.

Chapter Seventeen

Who are you people?" Cathy demanded. "Other than feral werewolves, I mean?"

Eric laughed arrogantly as he gestured around the warehouse. "We're the Master Race, of course."

He sounded like he really meant it.

"Of course you are," she told him.

His smile disappeared at her sarcasm. "You are one of us," he informed her. "Your place is by my side. You will be one of the mothers of a new breed destined to conquer the world."

The fanatical light in his eyes was nearly blinding, and she decided it was safer not to argue about it.

He unlocked her cage and brought another chair inside. "I have so much to tell you," he said once he'd taken a seat in front of her.

Cathy studied their positions and the distance to the open door behind him. Her chair was bolted to the floor of the cage, and her raw, bloody wrist was proof that the handcuffs weren't going to come off. About all she could do would be to kick Eric in the shins. While antagonizing him would be fun, what good could it do her at the moment? She'd play along with him for now.

"I've got the time if you want to talk," she told him.

"First, let me ask you a question," Eric said. "How much do you know about your Romany ancestry?"

She didn't want to discuss her personal life, but she suspected Eric knew more about some things than she did. "My mother didn't talk about her family."

"I can't blame her for wanting to deny her bad blood."

"You make her sound like a muggle or something."

He frowned, obviously not getting the reference. "Your family isn't from the typical rabble of gypsies. Your tribe have magic in their blood."

"So we're not muggles."

"During the war, scientists in the Reich discovered uses for the blood of your tribe. Much of the knowledge about the experiments was destroyed, but I am descended from a man who brought all the information that was left about werewolves to America." His chest puffed out proudly. "It's taken decades and three generations of volunteers to achieve the results my ancestor intended."

Cathy stared at him. "Let me get this straight—you *volunteered* to become a werewolf?" He nodded. She was appalled. "Why would anybody volunteer to turn into a mindless monster once a month?"

"Anyone who loves their race will gladly volunteer to defend it. My men and I are soldiers for our cause."

She'd been through a lot in the last couple of years—being turned into a monster, being rescued by a natural-born werewolf, being integrated into that werewolf's pack, discovering that the world contained not only werefolk but vampires and God knew what other kinds of supernatural beings—but this, this took the cake.

"I've been kidnapped by a gang of white supremacist werewolf bikers? Oh, for crying out loud!" she shouted. "There's only so much a woman can be expected to put up with, and I've had it up to here."

Eric merely smiled.

Cathy got herself under control. Just because

the situation was ridiculous, that didn't make it
any less dangerous.

"What did you mean, about the Hunyara having magic?" *And how do I use it against you?*

He grinned enthusiastically. "There's so much I
have to tell you. How long does it take for a bitten werewolf to learn to retain sentience during
the change?"

"We bitten can learn to control the murderous
rage eventually, but that's not the same as being
sentient in wolf form. Only natural-born werefolk are sane and themselves in human or animal
form."

"And yet you are already starting to come out
of the moonchange easier and faster than a normal feral, aren't you?" He grinned again. "And
how long does it take a bitten to learn how to
change form at will?"

"Never." Only those born as werefolk had
the skill to change from one form to another
whenever they chose. "A mortal who's bitten by
a werewolf is infected with a disease, not blessed,
like you seem to think." She lived with the disease every day, and it was this bastard's fault. Her
fingers curled, and she fought down a snarl.

"Your natural-born friends have told you
you're cursed. They are wrong, but they aren't
lying to you. You see, the natural-borns don't

know about the Hunyara strain of werewolf."

"Strain? That does sound like a disease."

"Perhaps I should have said the Hunyara breed. Your family has gone to great lengths to hide themselves from the natural-borns—who would destroy them. Ironic, isn't it, that you found yourself in the clutches of Michael Bleythin, the werefolk's fearsome Tracker? He'll execute you without a moment's hesitation if he finds out who you really are. He's a ruthless, pitiless defender of *his* own kind."

How dare this bastard talk about Mike like that? Mike had bent werefolk rules when he killed her maker but let her live.

"You'll be safe with us," Eric assured her. "I'll never let anyone hurt you."

She was chained and in a cage, so it seemed as if he was more interested in keeping himself safe from *her*. "And in turn for this protection, I give you what?"

He gave her a salacious once-over. "Offspring."

"That's what I figured."

"And the other Hunyara gifts you don't yet know you have. The Hunyara and the Movement have so much shared history."

She feigned enthusiasm. "Tell me about the Movement."

"Of course, much of our research was lost

because of a partisan raid of our facility during the war. Your ancestors who were being used as specimens escaped during that raid, and mine had to start looking for viable subjects all over again, in a new country with very little support. We had to hunt your family for decades. The Movement wasn't even aware of the existence of natural-born werewolves when research began in America. We had to learn the same caution as the Hunyara to keep our efforts secret from the natural subrace."

Cathy didn't think this guy had any clue how disturbing the things he said actually were. He was so *proud* of the current success of these experiments, and the means and results obviously didn't matter.

"The natural-borns will be the first subrace we destroy. There can only be one dominant wolf pack."

She understood pack hierarchy and territoriality with every fiber of her being. She also knew deep in her being that this loser's pack wasn't going to be the one that came out top dogs.

"You have a great-aunt Maria," he went on.

"Never heard of her."

"Your family thinks she died in a car crash. She was the first werewolf we managed to capture. I should say that she was the first Hunyara;

we succeeded in capturing a feral in the early seventies. We began to build our army from this stock. Your aunt managed to teach all the recruits to obey orders while changed into wolves. But only the offspring she bore learned the ability to change at will. We needed more Hunyara, so Maria's three sons took on the task of tracking down more of your family. They found the Hunyara living in Los Angeles."

"Sofia's family," Cathy guessed.

Eric nodded. "Our men would have brought Sofia to us when she was still a child, but it turned out that one of the old wolf tamers was still alive. Our people died, and Sofia and her family disappeared."

What a shame.

"But we were patient. A new generation grew up; we learned more. And now we have you. Soon we'll have Sofia. Then a new day will begin for the Master Race."

One of Eric's minions came up to the cage. "Walt's here."

Eric's manic smile grew even wider. "Now we can get started." He stood and gestured a newcomer over.

Cathy didn't like the looks of this Walt at all. He was big and blond and gorgeous, about six feet four inches of hard-muscled Teutonic perfection. Worst of all, he had the burning gold eyes of an überalpha wolf. There was nothing natural about his scent. Walt reeked of deadly danger, and cold calculation. If Eric was the brains of this operation, Walt was the enforcer. Walt sent a jolt of terror through her.

"What do you mean by 'get started'?" she asked.

Eric pulled her cell phone out of his pocket. "Show her," he said to Walt.

While Eric pressed buttons on her phone, Walt took off his clothing.

A fear worse than of being raped gripped her when he did something completely unexpected. Before her eyes, the huge human male turned into a yellow feral werewolf.

She'd often watched natural-born werewolves shift shape, but seeing a bitten do the impossible brought a scream to Cathy Carter's throat.

Chapter Eighteen

Jason stood outside Sofia's room for a few minutes before he knocked. He would have heard her frustrated shout even if his hearing wasn't better than a mortal's.

She flung the door open with such force that it bounced against the wall and flew back to hit her in the shoulder. "Ow! Don't you understand the word *leave*?"

Despite Sofia's very real fury, her eyes were happy to see him. He refrained from kissing her, putting his hands behind his back to fight other temptations as well.

"I do understand, and I will go," he told her. "I need to explain something first. May I come in?"

"No."

Had he been the traditional vampire of fiction,

that one word would have kept him from crossing her threshold. He stepped inside.

"I want to tell you something."

She backed up, and he saw her considering throwing the phone in her hand at him. Instead, she tossed it on the bed and rested her fists on the lovely curve of her hips. She'd gotten dressed, which he thought was a pity since he loved her naked body. Still, her tank top did a very nice job of outlining her bosom and slender waist.

"If you're done looking at my rack," she said after a long pause and a significant rise in the room's temperature, "I suggest you say what you have to and go."

"I'll never be done looking at you," he told her.

His response caught her between a smile and a grimace and he took another step closer. *Stop that bonding!* he ordered himself.

Jason forced down the lust and said, "I want to explain to you why I'm protecting you and teaching you, and generally interfering in your life."

"It's something about keeping a promise, right?"

"I'm a Prime of my word."

"What the hell's a Prime, anyway?"

"First things first."

With that, he moved forward and touched her.

* * *

"This month has to be better than last month," Jason said to Grigor. "We lost three during the last moonchange, and I'm sorry for it."

"What an odd Prime you are," was Grigor's answer. "Those beasts could never live as men; I'm not sorry for their deaths."

"I don't mind killing," Jason said. "I relish what I can do to the enemy. But I do hate having to destroy those who have already been victimized."

Grigor nodded. "My father made a wise choice when he chose to reveal our secrets to you."

"I may be a friend, but I'm not as effective an ally as I'd like to be."

"You've been a great help in training the ferals. I'm certain Maria and Yaros will be able to control the change on their own this month. We'll find out come sunset, I suppose."

Tonight was the first night of the full moon. Jason had been with the Hunyara for three months now.

"And," Jason continued, "my most pressing concern is that I didn't get all of the Nazi bastards responsible."

"We burned down the camp, and the bodies of every German that was there."

Jason nodded. "But partisan intelligence thinks that the top-ranking officers weren't in camp that night. I didn't notice any of the bodies wearing a uniform with a higher rank than captain."

"Half of them were in their pajamas." Grigor chuckled. "Though I suppose German officers would be the sort to wear their medals to bed."

"I'm not sure the civilian scientists were—"

"You have trouble, my friend," Grigor's father said as he came into the hut.

Jason knew instantly that he wasn't talking about werewolves. "He's found me." He stood. "I have to go. I'm sorry, but I can't be of any more help to you."

"You don't think we can stand against a vampire?" Grigor asked.

"No, you can't. And there is no reason for you to. I won't put anyone else in harm's way because of something I did."

"Very noble," Grigor said, putting a hand on Jason's shoulder. "Are you sure you're not a Clan Prime?"

He shook his head. "I almost wish I was. Then maybe I wouldn't be in so much trouble. How close is he?" he asked the Rom patriarch.

"I've had my people searching for a vampire's scent since you arrived and today is the first sign we've had. How he got this close without our knowing, I don't know. I wanted to give you an early warning."

"I'm grateful."

"After all the help you've been to us, do you think we'd let you just run?" Grigor asked. "We've planned for this."

Jason was appreciative of his friends' loyalty and kindness, but he had no intention of putting them in danger. "It's only an hour until sunset. I better go."

"You can't travel now," Grigor protested.

"It's a cloudy day and the woods are thick," his father said. "If you're careful, you'll be all right, Jason." He spoke to Grigor. "We'll set up our ambush to cover Jason's retreat."

Jason looked from one Rom to the other in shock. They looked back with stubborn determination. He knew they couldn't stop a vampire, and so did they. He also knew arguing with them would do no good. There was no way he could express the gratitude that filled him.

"What's your plan?" Jason asked.

"To buy you as much time as we can," Grigor answered. "Come nightfall and the moonchange, we'll set the German ferals free on your hunter. If he kills them, he'll be doing us a favor."

The enemy soldiers who'd allowed themselves to be bitten by captured werewolves and brought out of the camp with the rest of the moonchanged pack weren't interested in the training the Hunyara and Jason offered. The Hunyara were being kinder to these prisoners than the Germans had been to them, but kindness could only go so far during wartime.

"Crazed ferals won't slow a vampire down for long," Grigor went on. "But the sane members of the pack can lead him on a long dance after the ferals have tired him out a bit."

"We'll give you at least a few hours' start," the old man said.

"I'll take whatever you can give me," Jason answered. "And I want you to know that if you ever need my help again, I'll do whatever I can for your people."

Both men nodded, solemnly accepting this offer.

With that, Jason gave them each a quick hug, put on his heavy, hooded coat, and stepped out into the excruciating light of day.

Chapter Nineteen

You were being chased by a vampire?"

He ignored her skepticism. "That's not the point."

This man kept showing her the craziest things, but what the hell did it all mean? "Why were you being chased by a vampire?"

He brushed his thumbs across her temples. "I was being chased by a vampire cop, if you must know."

Sofia tried to take this in, and not be distracted by his gentle touch. "I'm still not sure I believe in werewolves; now you're adding Dracula to the mix. Why was Dracula after you?"

"His name is Matthias, not Vlad Dracul, and your family put themselves at risk to keep him from capturing me."

"But why . . . ?"

He sighed. "Because I did the wrong thing for the right reasons. The point is, I wanted you to know why I'm protecting you, why I'm training you. I made a promise to the Hunyara and I keep my promises."

She understood why he would be indebted for their trying to keep him from being captured, but he seemed to expect her to find her family's behavior admirable.

Sofia shook her head.

"You don't get it, do you?" she asked Jason. "You were a fugitive, and they helped you avoid capture. People who commit crimes are not sexy outlaw heroes—they are evil. People who help them are wrong. Wrong, wrong, wrong! I don't care that you're sworn to protect me now, because they helped you then. It's not my job to give you redemption, or pay your blood debt."

Jason took a step back. "Whoa. You don't have to be so melodramatic about it."

"I'm Rom and Hispanic—drama comes naturally." Actually, she'd been living a quiet life and avoiding drama for years. Jason brought out the unwanted wilder side of her nature, which was another good reason to get him out of her life.

"Now that you know that I don't find your

vows and crimes to be romantic, will you please leave?"

"Would it help if I told you your family's sacrifice didn't do me much good? Matthias caught up with me a week later, and I spent the next twenty years in prison."

The shadow that came into his eyes when he told her this twisted her heart. No, no, no! She was not going to feel sympathy for any con. Or any ex-con, no matter how fascinating and sexy she found him to be.

"Stop trying to manipulate me."

He sighed. "Point taken. That wasn't fair."

"Besides, don't you have to go feed your wolves, or something?"

"Thank you for thinking about them."

He seemed genuinely pleased, and when he touched her cheek, the ice around her heart nearly melted.

"All right, all right, I'm going," he said after they stood looking at each other for an unknown time.

The next thing Sofia knew, Jason was gone, but she had no memory of his leaving her room. She didn't remember the kiss either, but she still felt the effects of it, from the tingling top of her head to her toes curled on the thin motel carpet.

"Whew." She touched her sensitized lips and

sat weakly on the bed. Only when her hand brushed across the cell phone there did she recall what she should be doing.

"Sorry, Cathy," she murmured contritely. "With that man around, I can't seem to keep my mind on your emergency."

Cathy shut her mouth. Her panicked scream didn't last more than a few seconds but left her terribly embarrassed. Werewolves might howl occasionally, but Cathy hated being caught screaming like a girl.

So she glared at the captors staring at her and asked, "How the hell did he do that?"

Eric smiled at her with proprietary pride. "It's your right to know, Hunyara."

"My name's Carter," she said as the feral changed back into human form with the same ease as when he'd become a wolf.

This time she didn't scream, but she did watch his transformation carefully. Somehow her muscles seemed to almost understand the process. She'd never had this response when watching any of the Bleythin brothers change their form. She needed to learn this! She needed time to think about it, and to practice. She had to get out of this cage.

She looked to Eric. Damn, but she hated asking

anything of this bastard. "Tell me." She wasn't quite ready to say "Show me."

He still regarded her with that smug smile. "Research has revealed that, like any mortal, those with the Hunyara mutation must first be bitten to activate the changes that make you special. Once bitten—"

"Twice shy," she grumbled.

His smile widened somehow, and he made a gesture with his empty hand that took in her whole form like a distant caress. The naked guy looked her over as well, his eyes shining with hunger. Her hackles would have risen were she in wolf form. Still, she was unbearably curious.

Eric sensed her interest. "Can you guess why the Hunyara are different? Do you want me to tell you?"

The other feral's hand landed on Eric's shoulder. He seethed with impatience. "What about the other female?"

"Soon," Eric told him. His gaze never left Cathy.

Cathy finally gave in to that look. "Go on. Please."

"Vampires," he answered. She gaped, and he laughed. "Yes, you have vampire blood in you as well as werewolf."

"Not possible," she said.

"Vampires mate with mortals."

"Yeah." Among her friends and coworkers were Laurent and Eden, a vampire and mortal couple. "But vampires do not mate with were-wolves." She wrinkled her nose. "That would just be wrong."

She'd never been attracted to any vampire she'd met, and both Sid and Joe had told her that it wasn't possible for the two of them to be more than just good friends. Really, really good friends who gave each other longing looks when the other wasn't looking, from what she'd observed.

"The researchers want more proof," Eric went on, "but we think that once upon a time a vampire and a werewolf produced a child and began the Hunyara line."

"I realize you're trying to impress your future mate," the shifter said. "But I came here to collect the second female."

"I know," Eric said, and flipped open the cell phone. "You have quite a few voice mails," he told Cathy. "The natural-borns are quite anxious to have you back under their influence."

"You mean my friends are worried about me."

"Your cousin certainly is. Sofia has left as many messages as all the others put together. Family is so important, isn't it?"

Cathy sneered, "I suppose the plan is for me to call Sofia so you can lead her into a trap. I don't care what you threaten me with, but I won't do that to family."

Eric shook his head. "Trust you with a telephone? I don't think so." He began pressing buttons on the cell phone's keypad. "Not when text messaging can be used to trap her instead."

Chapter Twenty

Jason left the motel reluctantly, but Sofia was right about George and Gracie needing some attention.

"I'm sorry this isn't the vacation I promised you," he told the wolves when he let them out of the pen in the back of the SUV.

They jumped down to the crumbling parking lot concrete and George let out a howl while Gracie bumped her head against Jason's thigh. He rubbed her head while carefully looking around the area one more time. Sunlight warmed the cracked concrete and reflected off the pastel walls of the single-story motel buildings that stood on three sides of the parking lot. The street beyond was lined with almost identical motels and fast-food restaurants. The traffic moving by was light. It was all very worn-down and sad. He caught no sense of danger yet, but knew it was coming.

"Come on," he said to the wolves, and set off on a run with the animals at his side. Running with the wolves was good for him. They were mortal and he had to keep pace with them, because they could not keep up with him. Continual practice in being among mortals was necessary. And now he had a mortal woman to protect and cherish and bring into his world.

Kicking and screaming, no doubt. Jason smiled.

After a few more blocks he stopped at a fast-food place and bought a lot of hamburgers. He fed most of the burgers to the wolves, who complained because they preferred their meat raw. Then he headed back to the motel.

Once again he had to leave George and Gracie penned up in the SUV, but it was safer for them this way. A small generator provided them with air-conditioned comfort, which he envied as he climbed onto the roof over Sofia's room in the blistering Southern California sunlight.

There, Jason closed his eyes and opened his mind.

Sofia's restlessness reached him first. And the awareness that she missed him. He couldn't help but smile. What was righteous indignation at his supposed sins, compared to the draw of the bond?

She was stubborn, and determined to see the world in terms of black and white and right and wrong. She'd put him firmly into the black and wrong categories—but down there in her lonely room, she wished he was there.

The same way he wished to be with her. How much better it would be if they spent the day making love. She wouldn't be so self-righteous once he'd worn her out with hours of pleasure beyond bearing, now, would she?

After allowing himself a few moments of smugness, Jason tamped down that part of his Primal nature and went back to shameless telepathic spying on the woman he was sworn to protect.

Chapter Twenty-one

"Do you want to know what she has to say about Dracula on her blog?" Eden asked.

"No." Sid looked up from her computer to glance around the office of Bleythin Investigations. Eden was at her desk researching Sofia Hunyara, and Daniel sat on a chair behind Cathy's. He held something belonging to their missing friend cupped in his hands and closed his eyes as he psychically searched.

Joe, Mike, and Harry were off checking out an address out in the desert where Cathy had been asked to meet with some mysterious relatives.

Laurent was still following his own line of investigation, and hadn't checked in by telephone or telepathy for quite a while.

"The place seems so empty," Sid said.

"But at least no one's shedding on the furniture." Eden sighed. "I miss my husband and kid. At least Antonia is having a good time babysitting her only grandchild."

"I heard the slight emphasis on 'only.' Don't you start, too," Sid complained. "I'm working on the baby thing."

"With David Berus?"

Sid did not want to get into this subject. "So, what does this Sofia person have to say about Dracula?"

Eden cleared her throat and assumed a pedantic tone. "I quote from the wisdom of Sofia Hunyara: 'When I first read the book, I thought Stoker was the worst writer in the history of the English language. The story was full of too many characters, too many plot holes, and far too much overblown prose.

" 'Of course, I was thirteen at the time. Reading the book again after puberty set in, I came to the revelation, "Oh, that's what it's about." Why didn't the guy just say all that exchanging of fluids between dark foreign strangers and fair English flowers was about forbidden sex?

" 'I now understand what makes the story so timeless and evocative, but it's still full of plot holes. And why must there be fanatically loyal gypsies running around doing this vampire's bidding in Stoker's book? Why are Romany always portrayed as being on the side of the Dark Occult Powers in Western literature?' "

Eden stopped reading and chuckled. "I hope I meet this Sofia Hunyara sometime, so I can fill her in on the real history of vampires."

Sid boggled at her ex-vampire-hunter sister-in-law. "Are you saying Stoker *didn't* have it all wrong?"

"I'm not sure you have a need to know on that one, oh, Daughter of the Clan." She scrolled through several more screens of Sofia's blog. "She's really into old writers. She goes on and on for pages about *The Scarlet Letter.* I thought that was a Demi Moore movie."

"You don't read anything that isn't put out in comic book form from Marvel."

Neither did Laurent. Sid had even heard her brother and Eden refer to each other fondly as Gambit and Rogue.

"I'm a geek, I'm entitled. And don't tell me you've actually read *The Scarlet Letter.*"

"Point taken. Tell me, does any of what this woman says bring us any closer to finding Cathy?"

"Probably not," Eden replied. "But you're

right about the place seeming empty, and I'm try-ing to keep my mind off worrying about Cathy while we wait to hear from the guys."

"Me, too. My research isn't getting anywhere."

"What are you researching?"

"Not what, but who. I'm trying to figure out what Jason Cage has to do with all this. Not that there's much about him in the data I can access. Not without bringing a liaison between the Clans and Families into this already overpopulated mess."

"Why not call up the Caeg Family Matri? Aren't the vampire Clans and Families close allies?"

"We're close because we make a point of staying out of one another's business as much as possible. You saw how Jason had to ask permission to hang out in Clan territory, but didn't explain to the Matri what he's doing here, and she didn't press him for details."

"I wasn't actually there for that."

"Right. Oh, mighty hunter." *And please tell me he's decent genetic material,* she added to herself.

Eden looked thoughtful and rubbed her chin. "Let's see, I know that the Caegs are the largest and most influential of the vampire Families. I think Jason is the grandson or great-grandson of the current Matri. He's from one of the Eastern European branches of the family that came to

America after the Communist takeover of their home territory." She rubbed her chin again. "There's something I should remember about him—something I read in his dossier that I thought was cool and romantic, but—"

"You have dossiers on all of us?"

"Not all of you," Eden responded calmly to Sid's outrage. "I never heard of you before we met, or Laurent, but I did know a little about Antonia. Mostly the hunters concentrate on keeping tabs on the Tribe vampires," she reassured Sid.

Sid couldn't blame the mortal vampire hunters for spying on the Tribes. Tribal Primes were nothing but bad news for mortals and immortals alike.

"So, what did you think was cool and romantic about Jason Cage?"

Eden thought for a few more seconds, tapping a finger on her chin. "Oh, yeah, I remember. He got into trouble for trying to stop World War II. I guess he telepathically brainwashed some high-ranking Nazi. That's the kind of interference my kind goes after vampires for. Good intentions or not, your kind doesn't mess with our heads and get away with it."

"Messing with people's minds is bad," Sid agreed. It was evil and wrong and not to be tolerated; she believed this with all of her being, even though she'd done it herself—with good intentions. At least she hadn't been caught.

"I can't believe the hunters let Cage get away with brainwashing."

"We wouldn't have, except that the Families sent their own cop after him and put him away in solitary for a good, long time. I remember thinking that he was all cool and tragic for trying to save the world and getting in trouble for it. He sort of combined the Clan Primes' idealism with the pragmatism of the Families."

The Clans could use a bit more pragmatism, Sid thought. Maybe Jason Cage's DNA could help with that.

"But what does his past have to do with our present situation?" she wondered.

"Well, Cage used to hang out with Romany," Eden said.

"This Sofia Hunyara is Rom, Jason Cage is involved with Sofia, and Sofia is Cathy's cousin. Maybe they kidnapped Cathy."

"We don't yet have any proof that Cage is involved with Sofia."

"I'm psychic; I—"

Her phone rang and she answered it instantly. "Harry! Have you found her?"

"I'm not sure what we've found," the senior werewolf partner of the firm said. "When we reached the house there was nobody here, but the traces left behind are like nothing I've ever smelled before."

Harrison Bleythin had the best nose in the business. Harry's twin, Michael, had the ferocity, and their younger brother Joseph was one tenacious scent hound, but Harry was the elite bloodhound of the pack.

"Tell me," Sid said.

"Werewolves have been all over the place. And mortals. And a vampire. Most of them are related to Cathy."

"We knew that her family had contacted—"

"The werewolves are kin to Cathy," Harry interrupted, speaking slowly and distinctly.

This made no sense. "Please, Goddess, don't let her have been biting people when we weren't looking."

"That isn't possible," Harry reminded her. "You know she hasn't been out of our sight once during her moonchange."

Sid had a moment of relief, for Mike's sake as much as Cathy's. Mike Bleythin had another job besides private detective. Among werefolk kind he was known as the Tracker. It was his duty to take down the ferals and rogue werewolves. He'd spared Cathy from execution once. Sid knew it would destroy him if he had to kill her after all.

"The werefolk and the mortals that were in this house are *all* blood relations to our Cathy," Harry said.

"I so do not understand that." Had Cathy lied about how she'd been turned into a werewolf? "Mike rescued her from a feral. Didn't he? What about the vampire scent? Anyone you recognize?"

"Male," Harry said. "Not Wolf Clan, that's all I can tell. There was also a pair of true wolves here."

"Jason Cage travels with wolves," Sid told him. "I knew he had to be involved! He's with Cathy's cousin Sofia."

"The mortal female's scent will be hers," Harry said. "The Hunyaras have scattered. There's a dozen trails we could follow. What do you think, Sid?"

"Jason and Sofia," was her immediate response. "My gut tells me they're the clue to finding Cathy. We can solve the other puzzles once we have Cathy home safe."

"Agreed," Harry said.

He hung up on her, but Sid sent a telepathic *Stay in touch* his way.

Chapter Twenty-two

Sofia read the text messages from Cathy again and shook her head. She didn't like this—whatever this was.

"Too much mystery," she grumbled.

First there'd been the crazy relatives and the sexy stranger attaching himself to her. Now the missing cousin had reappeared but was being obtuse.

My senses are just about on overload. Got to get it together. I've got to get it under control.

But why do I feel the sudden need to be the one that's responsible? I'm not an alpha type, I'm a lone wolf.

And why am I using that sort of analogy?

She paced the motel room restlessly, the tension building in her making her want to scream. She needed a clear head. She needed a plan.

Sofia did not for one moment believe that her cousin was on her way to meet her here.

She missed Jason, missed him with every thought and breath. She missed him with her soul and every cell of her body. She missed him so much she couldn't stop herself from picking up the pillow his head had rested on and breathing in the scent of him that lingered there.

"Crazy."

Maybe she'd been too hard on him.

And maybe this was no time to obsess over her personal problems. She had to make sure Cathy was all right before she let herself worry about Sofia.

She noticed her laptop sitting on the motel room desk and smiled. She knew of one sure way to focus her thoughts. She might as well use the time spent waiting to get her head in order.

She sat down at the desk and switched on the computer. "Thank goodness this place has WiFi," she said, and soon began to type.

"Well, look what just popped up on Live Journal."

"What?" Sid asked Eden.

"A fresh posting from our girl Sofia. Let's see

what she has to say. *While sitting here waiting for a werewolf—*"

"What?" Sid bounded to her feet.

"Hush." Eden waved her back down. "Listen. 'I can't help but think about Jane Eyre.' "

"What does Jane Eyre have to do with—"

Eden gave her a withering look, and Sid subsided.

" 'It's one of my favorite books,' " Eden read on from the blog posting. " 'I love Jane's strength of character, her independent spirit, her resiliency. I guess I've unconsciously identified with her—a poor orphan girl making her way in a cruel world, with pride and dignity intact, and all that.

" 'But I never understood her and Rochester. I never understood that whole "passionate soul mates meant for each other" rubbish.

" 'Rochester tried to trick her into marrying him when he already had a mad wife up in the attic (and btw, the first thing I said to the person I'm really writing about was a reference to Jane Eyre). Anyway, Rochester lied to Jane, tried to trap her into a bigamous marriage, fell apart and felt sorry for himself when his nefarious plan was thwarted, and just generally acted in an irresponsible, selfish fashion.

" 'I believe in honesty and restraint. Unbridled passion creeps me out.

" 'But, still—I think I'm beginning to understand why she couldn't stay away from him despite her own self-respect and pride. Jane couldn't stop herself from running back to Rochester. He called to her and she had to answer the call.

" 'Maybe when you love someone, you forgive them. Maybe pride and love have nothing to do with each other. Maybe Rochester couldn't help what he did because he needed Jane to be with him, no matter what. I begin to get it, this call of passion despite one's better judgment. It sucks.' "

"I wonder what she's talking about?" Eden asked.

"It sounds like the beginning of a bond to me."

Eden wasn't the only one who jumped at the sound of David Berus's voice. She hadn't seen, heard, or felt him come in, but there he stood, large and blond and handsome, beside Eden's desk.

He turned a smile on her. "I met Charlotte Brontë once; she was quite old at the time. The lady certainly knew what she was talking about."

"I thought Charlotte Brontë died young," Sid said.

"That was the cover story that took her out of the mortal world," David answered. "She was bonded to a Prime. So of course she understood about soul mates and passion."

He looked away suddenly, and an awkward silence stretched out.

Sid noticed Eden almost shrinking in on herself in the hope of not being noticed. Eden had been born into a family of vampire hunters, and mortal hunters were responsible for the death of David's vampire bondmate.

Back in the bad old days the hunters had concentrated on killing vampire females, knowing that few daughters were born to vampires and only female vampires could give birth to vampire children. Sid knew her people had good reasons for the protected, circumscribed lives led by their women, despite her rebellion against the old ways.

David Berus had survived the loss of his bondmate, but the scars of that loss on his soul were still there in his eyes when he looked at Sid again.

She fought the urge to hug him and say "There, there." If she let herself get close to him, Lady Juanita's plan to hook her up with this very admirable Prime might succeed. Oh, no, that wasn't going to happen. She had plans of her own.

"Do you think Sofia is bonding with the Cage Prime?" Eden suddenly asked.

Not until I get my hands on a paper cup full of his sperm, Sid thought.

"Lady Juanita thinks so," David said.

"Cage and Sofia just met, so if they're bonding that quickly, that means Cathy's cousin is strongly psychic," Eden said. "I wonder what Sofia's being psychic has to do with werewolves?"

"I bet it means something," Sid said. When David came to stand by her desk, she stood and almost moved backward. Instead, she kept the desk between them and asked, "What can Bleythin Investigations do for you, David?"

He smiled. "I'm hoping I can be of some help to Bleythin Investigations. Lady Juanita suggested I apply for a position with your firm."

She'd been afraid he'd say something like that. "She wants us to work together, does she?"

"You know she does." He moved around the desk to stand close beside her. "The question is, what do you want?" His voice was rich and deep, and utterly seductive.

She didn't respond to him at all, and almost wished she could. If only she could feel something for one of her own kind! Sid met his coffee-dark gaze and tried to let his searching look spark something inside her.

Nope.

Chapter Twenty-three

Sid tried to think of something to say, but thankfully the office door opened and her mother came bustling in with Toni in her arms.

"Mommy!" Toni called. The toddler held her arms out to Eden.

"You do know she can walk?" Eden asked as she came to take her daughter. Her actions did nothing to prove this as she balanced the girl on her hip.

"I know you're very busy, Eden," Antonia said. "But I thought you could use a Mommy break."

"You are so right," Eden said, hugging Toni close. She began to stroke her daughter's cheek.

Sid noticed the fond look David gave the women and child, which she thought was sweet.

But she didn't appreciate it when he put his hand on her shoulder.

She slipped away from his touch and approached her mother. She barely managed not to growl when David followed close behind her. Maybe she had been hanging out with werewolves too much.

"What's Danny doing?" Toni asked, staring hard at the man seated behind Cathy's desk. *Oh, he's time walking,* the little girl added telepathically.

When Antonia winced, David put a hand comfortingly on her shoulder and said to Toni, "Use your out-loud voice, honey. You have quite a gifted child," he said to Eden.

Antonia brightened with pride and grinned with anticipation. "You don't know the half of it. Show Mommy, Toni."

Toni obediently turned her head and bit her mother's thumb.

Sid caught the sweet scent of blood as Eden shouted in pain and almost dropped her daughter.

But she held on, and so did Toni, suckling like any proper baby vampire. Eden started to pull her thumb out of Toni's mouth, but after a moment she gave a contented sigh and let the girl draw small sips from the bite.

"Nothing as good as mother's blood," Antonia said.

Sid was totally confounded. "But Toni's not—one of us."

"She's a daughter of the Clan," Antonia stated firmly. "Lady Juanita and I have suspected she'd make the change, and when her baby teeth popped out this morning we were sure."

"But how?" Sid asked. "Children born to mortals and Primes are always mortal themselves."

"Not always," Antonia said. "Why don't you explain, Eden? Hunters understand the process, don't they?"

"Yeah. But I never expected my own kid would be—"

"Explain!" Sid demanded.

"Most children born from any kind of vampire matings are male," Eden said. "Vampire genetics are inherited strictly from the female side. So, a son born to a Prime and a mortal woman is going to be mortal."

"There have been exceptions," David said.

"Granted," Eden said. "Maybe five or six sons of mortal matings have gone Prime in the history of the world, and they all had really funky powers, but the odds are astronomical for a male to turn vampire. Daughters of mortals and vampires can make the change, but only if the girl's mother has a vampire somewhere in her own ancestry."

"I've heard of mortal women who made the change when they were bonded to a Prime," Sid said.

"But they still have to be descended from a vampire." Eden looked thoughtful, then she laughed. "Of course, I'm from a hunter family."

"Hunters and vampires have been mating as long as there've been vampires and hunters," David said.

"But we hunters don't like to talk about certain *special* relationships. It's anathema to admit that our enemies sometimes turn out to be our destined loves." She laughed again. "I wonder which one of my grandpas had fangs and his own opera cape?"

"Watch the stereotypes," Sid told her. "And congratulations."

Eden didn't look quite like she was ready to be congratulated on this surprise turn of events, but Sid wanted to crow with glee. The vampire population was dangerously small, so every female added to their gene pool contributed to the species survival.

"I have to tell Laurent," Eden said. She slipped her thumb from her daughter's mouth. "Mommy needs to leave Daddy a voice mail now."

"Why?"

"Because Mommy isn't a telepath like you are."

Before Eden could turn toward her desk, Daniel suddenly stood up. "We have to go," he announced. It took his eyes a moment to focus on all the people suddenly staring at him. "They need our help," he told them. "Their minds are"—he shook his head as if trying to toss something out of it—"being messed with."

"Who?" Sid asked. "When?" After all, Daniel's peculiar psychic gift was for reading the past.

"The Bleythins," he answered. "All of them." He was pale, and he shuddered and took a deep breath before he went on. "We have to help. Right now."

"What did you see?" Sid demanded. She was skeptical, but she didn't question his urgency or his belief.

"I'll tell you on the way," he said. He headed toward the door. "Hurry!"

Sid and Eden looked at each other. "Do we go with this?" Eden said.

"We go," Sid decided.

Eden kissed Toni's forehead and handed her over to the waiting arms of Antonia, then headed after Daniel.

David would have come with them, but Sid

pointed to her niece. "That is a future Clan Mother. She needs guarding, Prime."

"You are a future Clan Mother," he reminded her.

Sid showed him her fangs. "It isn't only Primes who can grow these."

"Sidonie, be polite."

"Sorry, Mom." She drew in her fangs and nodded curtly to David. "Prime of the Snake Clan."

Antonia put a hand on David's arm. "I trust my daughter to take care of herself. Let her go. Stay here with me."

He didn't like it, but said, "As the Lady Antonia wishes."

Thanks, Mom, Sid thought as gently as she could to her telepathically null mother, and hurried after Daniel and Eden.

Chapter Twenty-four

Sofia had never thought of herself as impatient, but right now the waiting was killing her. Her only consolation was knowing that not being patient might get her killed.

Maybe.

Suspecting that she was acting like a delusional idiot about to be made a fool of was also killing her.

Any minute now, Cathy will show up. She checked her watch. *She's five minutes late, so she'll show up any second now. And then I'll know that all this werewolf stuff is crazy family folklore, and I'll feel like an idiot for my current behavior.*

Or . . .

From her car, Sofia stared at the door to her room and tried not to think about the "or."

She checked her watch one more time, then saw movement out of the corner of her eye. It was large, slinking carefully from shadow to shadow, keeping close to the wall. It was padding very carefully forward, stealthy and purposeful.

Damn!

Her stomach clenched with fear and she wanted to scream, but she would not give in to automatic fear.

She watched the wolf's careful approach and was glad that she'd taken a walk all over the motel buildings and parking lot. She'd carefully touched every door, every car, leaving her scent everywhere just in case she needed to confuse a creature she'd hoped wasn't really coming and didn't really exist.

That's probably one of Jason's pets.

She shook her head and ignored the voice of sanity. The wolf she watched was bigger than George and Gracie combined. They were gray and white; this one's fur was yellow.

She also doubted that George and Gracie were capable of doing what this wolf did when it reached her door. It reared up on its hind legs and banged its head against the wood.

There was a wolf at the door, and it was knocking.

Okay, now she had a certain amount of proof

that werewolves were real. But she had no idea how to ask a monster about her cousin. So she waited, hand poised over her keys.

When the door went unanswered, the wolf snarled. Then it backed up, ran forward, and hit the flimsy wood with the force of a battering ram. The door flew inward and the wolf rushed in.

Sofia had the car started before the werewolf bounded outside again. She had the car in gear by the time the creature saw her. His head came up and their eyes met; Sofia froze in terror.

His soul was evil and cruel, and she'd looked into eyes like those before.

Though her brain might've been frozen, her foot stomped on the gas pedal. The car sped forward but the werewolf easily jumped aside. Sofia was barely able to jerk the steering wheel hard to the left before slamming into the side of the building.

The monster was nowhere in sight when she headed toward the street.

The doors of her car were safely locked, but that did her no good when the werewolf jumped through the rear windshield.

Hot breath burned across the back of her neck, and Sofia threw open her door and rolled out. She hit the pavement hard while the car continued to move out into the street. She heard the crunch of metal and squealing tires behind her as she took off in the opposite direction.

She dodged into an alley behind the motel, hoping that a truck had flattened her car with the werewolf inside it.

No such luck, she realized within seconds when she heard the creature racing up behind her. The sound of claws scrambling on pavement sent a chill up her spine.

I'm repeating history. I need to be out in the open, among people. That thing won't draw attention to itself by attacking in a crowd.

Repeating history?

"Damn it!" she shouted. Consumed by sudden fury, she turned to face the onrushing beast. "Look at me, you bastard!" Her voice had never been so full of command and conviction before.

The beast did. Their gazes met and it came scrambling to a halt a few feet away from her.

The animal snarled, baring huge fangs.

Sofia glared, putting a lifetime's worth of anger into it.

She felt power gather in her. It was like nothing she'd ever known before; she was in control here.

Keep your distance, she thought at the werewolf. *Sit, and stay. How dare you look me in the eye?*

The werewolf snarled and snapped. Its whole body shuddered in resistance to her command.

After long, tense seconds, it began to slowly sink to its haunches.

Sofia concentrated as hard as she could, beginning to tremble, sweat beading on her forehead.

The werewolf continued to stare at her, defiance boiling in its gold eyes, its hard will boring into her determination.

She began to grow cold, though sunlight flamed against her skin. A dark tendril of fear began to twine through her, and a voice began to whisper in her head. She could make out no words, but the sound was sinister and distracting.

She took a shaky step forward.

He was calling to her, wasn't he?

How did he get into her head?

Her own thoughts distracted her, and shadows came up dark around her.

The alley changed. She changed.

She slammed into the brick wall before she could stop herself, scraping her palms and jarring her arms from wrists to shoulders. She turned around and fell to her knees, putting her at eye-level with the wolf.

He had a big head, and huge teeth. His eyes glowed, cruel and fierce, and full of hunger.

His eyes glowed!

He began to move in for the kill.

Chapter Twenty-five

Sweetheart, you were doing so well, too, Jason thought as he jumped off the roof behind the werewolf.

He'd kept his fury in check while monitoring Sofia's confrontation with the werewolf. Pride and hope warred with anxiety until she absolutely needed him.

Now he gave in to the fierceness of his nature and grabbed the creature from behind. His claws dug into soft fur and tough skin as he lifted the werewolf high over his head. It snarled and bucked in his grasp.

He ignored the struggling creature while he looked at Sofia's blank expression. "Come back, hon. You're fine."

She blinked and shook her head. Then she

looked up at the werewolf before meeting Jason's gaze. Puzzlement and anger replaced the shadows of the past that had consumed and crippled her.

"Try again," Jason said, and dropped the werewolf.

It instantly leapt at Sofia.

He hadn't expected the animal to be so fast. When he grabbed it again, he broke its neck. It was inches away from Sofia's throat.

"Nobody touches that neck but me," he said as he dropped the werewolf.

Sofia looked from the body at her feet to Jason. "You killed him."

Jason took her by the shoulders and drew her close. He gave her a hard, tight hug, then turned her, keeping an arm around her waist. How good she felt next to him! She quivered with tension, radiated shock and growing disgust, but she didn't try to pull away from him. Whether she acknowledged it or not, she needed him as much as he needed her.

"Look," he said. He leaned so that his cheek touched hers. "Watch."

Her attention was riveted by the large body stretched on the concrete in front of them.

The transformation of the yellow wolf took place with quick, magical grace. Reality stretched and briefly blurred, and became different. The sharp muzzle and pricked ears melded into a human head covered in long blond hair.

The human body that emerged was hard-muscled and huge, the same size as the wolf's but a different shape. She could clearly see him breathing.

"He's not dead."

Sofia looked over her shoulder at Jason. "You didn't kill him?"

"It takes a lot more than a broken neck to take out one of the werefolk."

He let her stare at her unconscious attacker for a few moments. She shuddered and he pulled her closer. A police siren sounded in front of the motel.

"You wanted me to see it—him—change."

"You needed proof." He turned her to face him. "You needed to believe."

She closed her eyes for a moment. They flashed with anger when she opened them. "You knew I'd be attacked." She sneered, "You wanted the chance to act the hero."

"No!" Her accusation stung. "I gave you the chance to save yourself. To prove to yourself that you could—"

She tried to struggle out of his embrace. "You let me face that—" She gestured wildly toward the werewolf.

He realized that she was still on the edge of panic and nothing would be settled until she calmed down. And they weren't going to be alone for long; there was a great deal of excitement about the wrecked car out in the street. He heard people shouting about having seen a huge dog running from the wreck.

Jason let Sofia go and bent to sling the werewolf over his shoulder.

"What are you going to do?" she asked.

He didn't ask her to come with him, but was glad when she followed him to the other end of the alley. He'd left his truck parked where Sofia wouldn't notice it when she left her room. He carried the prisoner to the vehicle and shoved the werewolf inside the empty wolf pen. The wolves were happy to keep away from the prisoner.

"The lock ought to hold him when he wakes up," Jason told Sofia. "I can't question him until he comes around."

"We've got to find out what they've done to Cathy."

"Right now, we have to get out of here." He took her arm, but she shook him off before he could lead her to the truck cab. He gestured back toward the motel. "We don't need mortal inter-ference."

"I need my stuff," she answered, heading off.

He caught up with her. "Why?"

She gave him an angry look. "I need my laptop for school. I left it in my room. At least I wasn't stupid enough to have it in the car."

"Waiting in the car was a good plan," he told her. "I wondered what you were up to when I saw you running around marking the place."

She blushed.

"You did great, Wolf-Tamer-in-Training," he assured her. "And right now, you have to keep thinking like what you are and get out of here."

She shook her head. "Do you think I can afford to run off and leave what little I have? Even if I'm supposed to save the world, I'm still on a budget."

Jason supposed that telling Sofia that he could fulfill her every material wish wasn't the way to win this independent woman's heart.

"Fine," he said, and took her into an empty motel room, with the wolves following at their heels.

Once inside he couldn't stop himself from kissing her, and after a moment her mouth opened beneath his and her arms came around his back. They clung together in an eager, hot embrace for a few moments before Jason reluctantly drew away.

"I'll get your stuff for you. Stay right here," he ordered. "All of you."

"Wait a second," she insisted as he started to leave. He glanced back. Arousal stretched across the room between them. She touched a finger to her sensitized lips, but her gaze was sharply questioning. "How did you get that door open?"

He smiled. "It's just a little trick my people have."

"You're not a werewolf, right?"

"Right."

"I saw how fast you moved, how strong you are, and you've got all that"—she tapped her forehead—"telepathic talent. What are you?"

Jason knew he'd put this off too long, but he couldn't help but smile wider and show a great deal of fang. "I'm a vampire, sweetheart."

He closed the door behind him, but he still heard Sofia's stunned whisper. "Vampire?"

He laughed out loud as he ran toward her room.

Chapter Twenty-six

Sofia looked at the wolves that had jumped up on the bed. "He's a vampire. Did you know about this?"

Not that the wolves answered. They were, after all, just plain fierce, huge Arctic wolves, not vicious telepathic mean werewolf scum. One of them yawned at her.

She turned away from George and Gracie, unable to muster any fear of natural canines anymore.

Sofia began to pace around the small room, seething. She had to get rid of all the pent-up frustration and confusion somehow.

Not to mention anger. *I've got quite a few things to say to that man. Vampire.*

"What does he *mean*, he's a vampire?"

The wolves refrained from commenting.

Why did she believe him? And where was he? Why wasn't he back yet?

Oh, please, it's only been about thirty seconds.

Her back was to the door when the wolves began to howl. As she turned, they jumped down to cower beside the bed.

"Just what the hell do you think you're doing?" Sofia shouted at the three black werewolves that rushed through the doorway.

For the first time in her life, she was too angry to know any fear. "I am *not* putting up with this anymore!"

She swept them with a glare. All three beasts had bright blue eyes, full of intelligence. Sofia's were full of determined fury when she took them on. They surrounded her in an arc and began to stalk slowly forward.

She stomped her foot. "Oh, no you don't." She pointed to them one at a time. "Stay right where you are."

She repeated the order as a thought, a firm mental command spoken directly into their minds.

They froze.

Two of them looked surprised. The third growled and bared his fangs at her.

She felt him trying to change, and she stopped him. She wasn't sure how she did it, but the control came as naturally as breathing. They fought her, pushing at her mental control, and she pushed back. She smiled as the tug-of-war accelerated.

She was utterly and completely pissed off, and that was a good thing. Jason paused outside the door to savor the triumphant fierceness of his soul's equal. Her power and strength filled him with a pride and love he'd never experienced before. What a woman!

And she was his.

Every possessive fiber of his being insisted on the truth of their bonding.

But right now, police officers were going from room to room looking for the owner of the squashed vehicle in the street. A small crowd was gathered in the parking lot. Jason had already had an encounter with a female officer whom he'd telepathically convinced hadn't seen him, and that the room where Sofia waited had already been searched.

They needed to deal with the latest batch of werewolves, get back to the prisoner, and get out of here. He tucked her suitcase and laptop under one arm, and eased into the room.

Sofia didn't glance around when he entered, but all three werewolves growled. George and

Gracie whimpered from the far side of the bed.

"Wimps," Jason told his wolves. He looked at the big, black werewolves and spoke to the snarling one in the center. "Hi, Mike."

Mike Bleythin snapped his jaws angrily.

"We haven't been introduced, but I assume you two are Harry and Joe," Jason went on.

"Do you know these creatures?" Sofia asked without taking her attention off her captives.

"This is Sofia Hunyara," he told the Bleythins. "She's Cathy Carter's cousin, and I just now realized who Cathy must be."

"What do you mean?" Sofia asked.

Two of the wolves tilted their heads curiously, as well.

"I'll explain when we can all have a civil discussion."

He put Sofia's stuff down by the door and came up to put his arm around her slender waist. Her head barely came up to his shoulder, but her newfound strength of will filled the room.

"She's mine," he informed the Bleythins, who knew better than to mess with a vampire. "You can let them go, sweetheart," he told Sofia. "These are the good guys."

Sofia was trembling enough for him to feel it even as she showed a brave front to the werewolves.

"Good guys?" she questioned. "They're were-wolves! They broke in!"

"Which was quite rude of them," he agreed. "I'm sure they'll apologize if you let them turn back into humans."

It's all right, he whispered into her mind. *It truly is all right. They're Cathy's friends.*

She hesitated, but decided to trust him.

He held on to her when she let go of the mental leash. The rush of released energy would have knocked her to her knees if he hadn't been there to hold her. She closed her eyes and leaned her head against his shoulder, spent and breathing heavily.

It was too bad her eyes were closed, because she missed the quick transformation of Mike, Harry, and Joe, and the looks of shocked outrage they turned on the woman who'd held them at bay.

Jason smiled proudly. "Yep, she's good. Her people would call her a Wolf Tamer."

Chapter Twenty-seven

Jason's words were a soothing balm to her soul. She had a family. She had a place in the world. A purpose. And it was Jason who had brought her to this place.

But it was a stranger's angry shout of "What the hell is going on here?" that brought Sofia's attention back to the situation.

When she opened her eyes she saw three naked men. Large, well-made, black-haired men with the blue eyes she'd stared into when they were in wolf shape a few moments before. Two of the men looked so much alike they had to be twins. The third was younger and more slender, but enough alike the twins that he had to be their brother.

The one who'd shouted was standing right in

front of her, body tense, fists clenched. His fury was barely held in check, and for a moment she wanted to slink behind Jason.

She lifted her chin and asked the werewolf, "Are you really Cathy's friend?"

"I'm Mike Bleythin," he said. His next words were low and threatening. "I've never heard of a Tamer, but perhaps you've heard of the Tracker?"

Jason's embrace tightened protectively, but it wasn't the reassurance of his being there that kept her calm. Though she did appreciate having him beside her.

"No, I haven't heard of any Tracker. I just found out about werewolves, actually. I take it Tracker is a werewolf title," she said to Mike. "You haven't answered my question."

"What was your question?" Mike's twin asked. He shouldered his threatening brother aside. "I'm Harrison, the sane member of the family. Let's talk."

"We're looking for our friend," the youngest werewolf said. "So far, following the trail to you has been all we've been able to do."

"My lady was attacked by a werewolf before you arrived," Jason said.

"One of the Hunyara pack?" Mike asked.

"I seriously doubt it. A Hunyara would recognize a vampire's scent, but this feral had no clue I was around. Don't tell me you didn't pick up his scent? It must be all over the neighborhood."

All three Bleythins looked shocked. Harry shook his head. "Not a whiff."

"You're kidding."

"I wish we were. That's why we haven't been able to find Cathy. There's no fresh scent of her anywhere."

"What happened to this invisible werewolf?" Mike asked.

"I have him locked up in my Denali," Jason said.

The brothers exchanged looks. Harry spoke to Sofia again. "To answer your question, all of us are friends of Cathy's. More than that, we're her pack brothers. May I now ask you some questions?"

Sofia wanted more explanations, but nodded.

"Do you know why you were attacked?"

After thinking about it for a moment Sofia came to a dreadful conclusion. "He wanted to turn me into a werewolf." She looked at Jason. "Why would he do that?"

"I think I'll go ask him," Mike said, and suddenly the big naked man turned into a huge black wolf.

"Mi—" Harry began, but Mike was out the door before he could finish.

"He's the Tracker," Joe said. "Let him do his job."

Sofia waited for an explanation, but all Jason said was, "I hope he doesn't leave any blood in my truck."

Sofia decided she didn't want any more information. If she thought about it she might be sick, which she did not want to do in front of the werewolves.

Harry reclaimed her attention when he asked Jason, "What did you mean about knowing who Cathy must be?"

"I just remembered that the name of the woman Mike brought to my cousin's wedding was Cathy. I hadn't associated her with the woman Sofia is looking for, until the three of you showed up. To tell you the truth, I've been thinking so hard about not getting Mike involved in Hunyara business that I forgot he's based in San Diego."

Sofia's head spun with confusion once more. "Vampires have cousins? Werewolves go to weddings?" She looked into Jason's amused gaze and telepathically said *I don't know anything about your world.*

And now isn't the time to discuss it, he answered as the door burst open again.

* * *

Sid would not let Daniel drive.

"Becasue I've seen you do it with your eyes closed," she told him when he protested that he knew where they had to go.

Daniel gave directions while Sid sped her sleek black Mercedes skillfully through heavy traffic. He did it with his eyes closed.

"I hate having one more thing to worry about," Eden said from the backseat.

Sid gave a quick glance back at Eden's worried face. "I'm sure we can get the boys out of whatever trouble Dan's seeing."

Eden sighed. "I was talking about finding out my daughter's going to be a vampire."

Sid couldn't see this as anything but an occasion for rejoicing, but she tried to get a mortal mother's perspective on it. Especially a mortal who'd been trained to hunt vampires. She couldn't do it.

"You object to a miracle?" she asked after making a quick left turn at Daniel's direction. Tires squealed and horns blared in her wake.

"I can't object to biological fact," Eden said. "But I need some time to wrap my mind around it."

"We all do," Sid said. "As soon as we get Cathy home."

"Right," Eden agreed. "But Laurent and I aren't

your average vampire couple, and if Lady Juanita thinks we're going to raise our kid as a proper little vampire princess—no offense—"

"None taken."

"—she's got another thing coming."

"Spoken like a true hunter." Another turn. More offended drivers. At least no cops had noticed yet. "I'll do what I can to help. So will Antonia."

Eden reached forward to pat Sid's shoulder. "Thanks—we'll take all the help we can get. Speaking of Lady Antonia," she added, "I approve of that bit of matchmaking you pulled on her and that dishy Berus Prime, even if you did use my daughter as your excuse. Your mom could use someone nice."

Sid drove in flabbergasted silence. She'd only been trying to duck out on a date with destiny with David Berus herself. She hadn't been trying to dangle her own mother as bait to attract the Prime's attention away from herself.

Though come to think of it, that wasn't a bad idea.

No, no, no! Sidonie Wolf, you will not think like that!

Daniel broke in, "Traffic will be blocked up ahead. Turn right at the next light. We'll come around from the back." After a couple of minutes he said, "Left here. Stop."

She barely had the car parked behind a long, one-story structure when Daniel jumped out and ran toward the front of the building.

"I think his eyes are still closed," Sid said as she and Eden followed him.

She overtook him in a couple of steps, being faster and stronger and far more dangerous than her mortal relative. She felt Joe and the others' presence and she was the first one through the door, ready for any danger waiting inside.

Instead, the first person she saw was Jason Cage. She came to a quick halt and cheerfully said, "Hi!"

Chapter Twenty-eight

A new trio of people rushed in, led by a gorgeous blonde woman.

Somehow, Sofia was certain none of this trio were werewolves. She expected them to attack, but instead the blonde's eyes brightened at the sight of Jason and she looked like she wanted to eat him up.

Jealousy boiled through Sofia, but the woman took no notice of her.

Instead the blonde put her hands on curvy hips and looked at the naked men. "So, Harry, do you need rescuing, or is this about to turn into an embarrassing situation?"

"We needed rescuing about ten minutes ago," Harry answered.

"See, Dan's getting better," said the other

woman who'd come in. "He's up to seeing ten minutes into the past, instead of two hundred years."

When she heard the name Dan, Sofia looked hard at the blond young man wearing glasses and the striking woman with dark curls next to the tall blonde. Realization dawned at last.

She pointed at the dark-haired woman. "You're Eden." To the blonde. "And you're Sid. And Mike and Harry and Joe—I should have remembered about you when you told me your names. But having three more werewolves come at me scared me to death."

"You didn't act scared," Joe said.

"Oh, God, I'm sorry!" Sofia told her cousin's coworkers. "Cathy's told me all about you—except for the werewolf stuff."

"That's understandable," Sid said. "Except Cathy never told us about you."

"I'm sorry about what I did to your brains," Sofia said to Joe and Harry, carefully not looking below chin level.

Sofia wondered if she was the only one who cared that there were a couple of naked men in the room.

Not men, Jason thought at her, *werewolves. And I'd rather you didn't look at anyone but me.*

Right, she thought back.

She wouldn't mind looking at him naked. She didn't think Sid would mind, either. And why the devil couldn't she get her mind off having sex with Jason, when there were more important things to deal with?

This reminds me of a scene in A Night at the Opera, Jason continued in her head as the new-comers and naked men began talking among themselves. *More and more people and luggage and things keep piling into this tiny ship state-room, until eventually no one can move, and finally it's so crowded people start falling out the door.*

A Night at the Opera? she asked.

"It's a Marx Brothers movie," Jason explained. "It's a comedy from the 1930s."

"Oh." *I want to have sex with you,* she thought. *I know.*

I can't help it, and I don't like that I can't help it. You don't like the sex?

She very much liked the sex. She craved the sex. She wanted him covering her and inside her, and her body was burning just because his arm was around her. Why didn't these people go *away?*

I don't like this—compulsion. Is it because you're a vampire and drank my blood that I want you constantly? Anger sizzled through her, but the need for him didn't abate any. *Are you forcing me to feel like this?*

Sweetheart, I feel the same way you do.

While the others talked, Jason whirled her around into the bathroom and closed the door.

"I'm not going to kiss you," he said, though he held her close and she automatically pressed her body against his. He could feel the hard swell of her nipples through the fabric of her shirt. "Stop tempting me for a moment."

"How?"

"I don't know." He lifted her chin to look into her eyes even while the sweetness of her lips beckoned to him. "Although I very much want to kiss you, instead I'm going to tell you some things, and I want you to listen to me without any argument. Promise me that you'll listen and think about everything, and we'll discuss it or argue later."

"You're a vampire. A vampire ex-con. But everything you've told me so far has turned out to be true, so all right," she said. "I promise to keep my mouth shut and listen."

"I am a Prime, which means I am an adult male vampire. Vampires are people," he said. "Some vampires are good, some are bad, most are somewhere in between. We have our own cultures and history and problems. We aren't the dead brought back to life; we're born vampires. We don't turn people into vampires when we bite them."

"Only werewolves do that?"

"Right, but I'm explaining my own people now. We can't fly without airplanes, or change shape like the werefolk can. We do suffer from some of the problems you see in the movies— allergies to sunlight and garlic and silver and certain types of wood, but we take medicines for these allergies.

"We don't fear religious symbols. Or sleep in coffins, or need to rest in the earth of our home-land, or have trouble crossing running water.

"We are telepathic, we are faster and stronger and longer-lived than mortals. We do need to drink blood, for nourishment and for psychic reasons, and especially to enhance sexual gratifi-cation—but we don't have to kill when we taste mortals.

"I'm not saying we don't have tendencies for fierceness and violence, but we channel those tendencies—at least most of us do, most of the time—into acceptable pursuits. I control tigers for a living, for example.

"We're highly sexed and we love making love, to our own females and with mortal women. If we're very lucky, we find the one woman that is destined to be our bondmate. A bondmate is our perfect sexual and psychic partner, and we are the perfect partner for our bonded. The mortal term is probably soul mate.

"You are my soul mate, Sofia, and I am yours. You can deny it and fight it, but it is the truth. You want me, I want you, and every issue that stands in between is just bullshit. Normally we could and would work it out. But right now we have the complication of your being needed by your people, and my giving you up if I have to in order to fulfill my obligation to your people, and I have no idea of how we're going to get around that."

He paused. "You can talk now."

As she opened her mouth to say something, a knock sounded on the bathroom door.

"Come along, you two," Harry called. "It's time we got back to hunting for Cathy."

Chapter Twenty-nine

Cathy's captors kept spraying themselves and her with the stuff that blocked out scent. It made her eyes water and she kept sneezing. She knew an allergic reaction was the least of her problems. As time crept by, Cathy also tried to keep her mind off the bad things that could happen to Sofia.

Sofia was an innocent mortal in town simply to meet family. Cathy was terrified her cousin would walk into an ambush and be turned into a werewolf, just as she had been.

She tried to assuage her guilt over involving Sofia in this by envisioning all the ways she'd savage and mutilate her captors as soon as she broke free, but such thoughts only made her want to gnaw at her shackled wrist to facilitate her escape. Two things kept her from the stupid move. One was the fact that she was still a sane human being until the moon was full and not a raging, insane werewolf.

Come the full moon, though . . . She kept unconsciously smiling about that, and flexing her fingers as though they already sported strong, sharp claws.

The other drawback was that if she somehow managed to bite off her own hand, she would still be locked inside a cage. And oh, yeah, bleeding to death.

She tried not to believe any of the things Eric had told her about his plans, her people, and especially her werewolf and vampire friends. But his ideas gnawed at her.

Don't think about gnawing.

Her only distraction came from studying everything around her. There were a great many people coming and going from the warehouse. They were bringing in supplies and loading them into shiny new vans and trucks and Hummers, while Eric supervised and gave orders like a general preparing a campaign. Some of those supplies were weapons and ammo, which gave her a very bad feeling.

"What do werewolves need with guns?" she

asked as Eric strolled her way after slapping a subordinate.

"It takes more than werewolves to take over the world, darling," he told her.

"Superpowers have nuclear weapons," she said. "What have you got? Fleas?"

He grinned at her. "I take my Top Spot every month. We're working on getting the nukes."

Cathy's heart sank. "You're joking."

"Only about the flea medicine."

She got the distinct impression that he wanted her to be proud of his plans for world domination.

"Am I supposed to bat my eyelashes and say, 'Oh, you're so alpha'?"

He laughed. "Oh, no. I want you to know that I'm worthy of having an alpha bitch like you for myself."

In a werewolf way, this was the most romantic thing anyone had ever said to her. Mike certainly never—

"Do you really believe you and I are members of the master race?" she asked. "Or are you just power hungry?"

"Yes," he answered, flashing that sharp-toothed grin again. "And we won't *be* the master race until we wipe out the naturals and then the vampires, but one thing at a time. First we absorb the Hunyara genetics into our own. Then we must build up our ranks and expand our territory. We must gain more allies and exploit their weaknesses when they are no longer useful. The war hasn't begun yet, but the buildup is well under way." He looked at his watch. "I wonder what's taking Walt so long." He chuckled. "He's probably taking his time with a female he knows he's not fit to bed in her proper state. I would do the same, if I knew it was my only chance with an alpha female. Not that I'll let him breed her. Or you," he added to Cathy.

"I love it when you talk like that," she said, but doubted Eric recognized her sarcasm.

Their conversation was interrupted by the warehouse door swinging open to allow a new van to drive inside. Eric went over to greet the newcomers.

"We got a couple of them!" a bearded man shouted as he got out of the van. He gave a triumphant laugh. "It was as easy as you said it would be. All we had to do was follow those natural-borns and they led us to the Hunyara hideout. After the naturals gave up and left, a pair of Hunyara males came slinking back to the house. They're as feral as we are and put up a good fight. We stunned them and came straight here." He glanced toward a second man who'd come around from the passenger side and looked sheepish. "Well, not quite straight back."

"I stopped for a girlfriend along the way," the other man said. He faced Eric squarely, making eye contact for a few crucial seconds. When Eric didn't slap him down, he went on. "Nobody saw the pickup. She won't be missed. We can always eat her if she doesn't take to being turned."

Cathy fought down the urge to throw up.

"We sprayed everybody down mostly," the first man went on.

"What the hell does that mean?" Eric demanded.

"We ran out of deodorant, but not until everybody'd been sprayed," the other man answered. "At least enough."

"Define *enough*?" Eric asked, voice low and threatening. All activity had stopped, and his people stared at him. "Pack up," he ordered. People sprang into action without any questions, while Eric turned his attention back to the newcomers. "That was good work snatching the Hunyaras," he said, getting grateful looks from the pair. "But did it occur to you that the natural-borns might have returned to the Hunyara house, too? Maybe they're trailing the Hunyaras right now. If they are, and there's the faintest trace of scent to follow, you'd be leading them back here."

Cathy could only hope.

The driver shook his head. "No way. We got the stink off of all of us. But it wouldn't hurt to spray everything down again anyway."

"You do that," Eric said. "Everything and everyone." He rubbed his hands across his face and rolled his head to relieve tense muscles. "Things are moving faster than I'd like, but we'll be okay." He gestured two men over. "Tanner, I want you to get the caravan moving north, right away. Call Nathan when you're out of the city to give an update on the situation. Make sure you get the Hunyaras back to base in good shape. John, your team and two vehicles will remain here with me. Make sure at least one of the team can operate the vampire zapper, and break out some silver rounds for one of the modified AKs. We've got one more delivery. I'll wait here for it. Send out a couple of men to track down Walt."

Cathy did not like this evidence of her captors' efficiency.

Tanner gestured toward her. "Do we take her?"

"I'm not trusting transporting the bitches to anyone but me. Get moving."

Cathy watched the increased activity with growing dread. One of the men came over and sprayed her cage full of the deodorant chemical, and she started to cough and sneeze, her eyes watering so much that everything became blurred.

To get her mind off the discomfort, she focused her attention deep inside. Maybe, if she tried hard enough, she could figure out how to shape-shift on her own before the full moon forced the change—whether she wanted it or not.

Chapter Thirty

You didn't have to break into my truck," Jason complained as Mike entered the office. "I would have given you the keys."

The big werewolf ignored the Prime and looked Sid's way. "Status?" he growled.

She was more interested in what Mike might have learned, but she saw that he wanted time to get his seething anger at Jason under control. Since he was a dear friend, and she didn't want the office wrecked if the Tracker and Prime got into it, she answered his question.

"Harry and Joe decided to follow the trails of any Hunyara werewolves they can find."

"None of my relatives know where Cathy is, either," Sofia spoke up. She was sitting at Cathy's desk, with Daniel standing next to her.

"But we'd still like to talk to them," Sid told her.

"Oh, yes," Mike said softly, focusing his blue laser stare on her. "I certainly intend to talk to them."

Fear crossed the mortal's face, followed by a flash of determination. Sid wondered if Mike was deliberately trying to make an enemy of a woman who could control werefolk. More than likely he was still upset about what he'd had to do to the feral werewolf, and was taking it out on Sofia.

"What do you mean by that?" Sofia demanded of Mike.

"Daniel has been showing Sofia what he does," Sid continued quickly. *Keep it together, Tracker,* she sent telepathically. "And Sofia and Jason have been trying to see if the glimpses of the past he pulls up make any sense to them."

"Nothing so far," Daniel said.

Mike continued to glare at the mortal. The Prime didn't like it. Damn, this could go bad.

"Still no word from Laurent," Sid went on. "I sent Eden home to be with Toni—more on that situation later. And I have been catching up on our casework while waiting for you." *I have also been telepathically looking for Cathy,* she telepathically told Mike. *But I think whoever has her is using a psychic damping device like the vampire hunters use.*

Do you think those Purist bastards have her?

I certainly hope not. Are you calm enough to talk yet?

"No." Mike turned toward Jason. "Why the hell didn't you tell me about these Hunyara ferals?"

Jason rose and faced the Tracker's fury quite calmly. "They're a very private people, and it's not my story to tell. What did *you* find out from the feral?"

"*Everything* about werefolk is my business," Mike growled. "What am I supposed to tell the governing council about a gang of mavericks we've never heard of before? What do we do about them?"

"The Hunyara aren't the problem," Jason said. "It's the ferals that are preying on the Hunyara that are our problem. What did the feral tell you?"

Mike's fists clenched at his sides. "My species has been put at risk and—"

"Cathy! Remember her?" Sofia suddenly put herself between Mike and Jason. "I thought you cared about her. I know she cares about you, but you aren't doing anything at the moment to show me why she should."

Mike's attention switched to the small mortal

woman, and the tension that flowed between them filled the room.

Sid saw how Jason prepared to spring forward to protect his woman. She admired the Prime's effort at restraint. He had Sofia's back, but encouraged her independence. She liked that in a Prime, especially since it didn't come naturally to them.

At least a minute stretched out before Mike scratched his jaw and nodded to Sofia. She nodded back. Air came back into the room, and Jason stepped forward to put his hand on Sofia's shoulder.

The opening chords of Coyote's "Tempting Fate" began to play, and Sid quickly answered her cell phone. That was the ringtone she'd programmed for Tony Crowe.

Everybody looked her way.

"Hi, Dad. I can't talk right—"

"I asked Dr. Casmerek about that thing you wanted to know about," Tony interrupted. He sounded cranky. "I didn't like it, but I asked."

"Thank you." She couldn't keep from looking Jason over. Sofia noticed. "What was his response?"

"He said it's possible. He wants you to give him a call. Don't."

"You know I have to."

"You're a stubborn child."

She wanted to dance with elation. She wondered if Jason would let her lead. She smiled. "Thanks for doing this for me. I'll get back to him as soon as I can."

"What's that about?" Mike asked when she hung up. Werewolves' hearing might possibly be better than vampires.

"Nothing involved with any of our cases," Sid answered. She folded her hands on top of her desk, all prim, proper, and professional. "What did you learn from the feral?"

Mike concentrated on Sofia. "He was sent to bring you over to his kind, the way they did with Cathy. They want female ferals."

"I suggest you moderate your tone," Jason said. "You sound like you're blaming the victims."

Mike gave Jason a long, hard look, but went on coolly. "He didn't know where they're keeping Cathy. They kept him out of that loop by blindfolding him and driving him everywhere—just in case he got caught. I learned a lot of things from him, but not how to find Cathy. We'll discuss those things after we find her," he told Sofia.

Chapter Thirty-one

Sofia did not like this guy, and couldn't see why Cathy constantly raved about Mike in her e-mails. Okay, he was big and strong and handsome, but he wasn't very nice. Was Cathy's life in danger from him now?

"Do you want to find her because she's your friend, or because she's a danger to your species?"

Mike walked away without answering and went to talk quietly with Sid.

Sofia watched him carefully, worried.

On the drive to the Bleythin office, Jason had told Sofia what he knew about natural-born werewolf society, and how hard her family had worked to keep their existence from the natural-borns. He explained that the werefolk consisted of all sorts of shape-shifting predators—foxes, cougars, bears, and more—but werewolves were at the top of the food chain. The natural-borns were a paranoid lot with *rules,* and Mike Bleythin's job was to enforce them.

Though she was new to the idea of having a family, she'd developed a fierce need to protect all the Hunyara. Now she might have to protect them from Mike Bleythin, the Tracker, as well as from these ferals out to use the Hunyara family for their own purposes.

"Cathy first," Jason said.

He put his arm around her waist and she drew comfort from being near him, comfort from the way he knew her mind.

"I wish we hadn't come here," she whispered to Jason.

For one thing, she didn't like the way Sid kept looking at Jason with blatant, hungry interest that sent waves of jealousy through her.

I'm not interested in her, Jason thought at her.

You're flattered, though, she thought back.

I can't help it, sweetheart. I'm a Prime, and she's a female of our species. We Primes are vain—we love it when the ladies take notice. It doesn't mean anything.

Maybe not to him, but it sure distracted her. Finding out that Sid Wolf was also a vampire had shocked her, but she adjusted to the idea quicker than she would have a few hours before.

Detaching herself from Jason's touch—and bothered by how hard it was to do—she went back to stand by Daniel. Jason went over to Mike and Sid.

"Tell me about your father," Daniel said when she reached him. He adjusted his wire-rimmed glasses on his nose. "He and Cathy's mother are twins, aren't they? Multiple births are common in werefolk families."

"My *father*. Oh, my God!"

Sofia staggered to a seat as the room spun sickeningly around her. She was vaguely aware of Jason coming toward her, and of his turning to face the door when it opened.

She knows, Jason realized. Sofia's heartbreak ached in his chest. Her head dropped into her hands and he could almost taste the sudden tears welling from her eyes.

But when a pair of vampires entered, he automatically put himself between his mate and any potential danger. He relaxed when he recognized Sid's mother and the Snake Clan Prime he'd met at the Matri's party.

Sofia looked up, wiped the back of her hand

across her eyes, and put her feelings aside. Jason admired her resilience, but feared someday she was going to break apart.

"I came to renew my offer of help," David Berus said.

Sid stood and gave the Prime a wan smile. "Thank you. And Mom—"

Another Prime came through the doorway before she could finish. He radiated excitement and all eyes turned his way.

"Laurent!" Sid said eagerly. "You've got something."

"Who's the elf lord?" Jason heard Sofia ask Daniel.

"I think we're beginning to need a flowchart," he whispered back.

"I've got some information," the newcomer said. He flashed a charming smile at Sofia. "Don't be alarmed, miss, I work here. If I take the time to hit on you, as politeness requires, my sister over there will be annoyed, so I'll get on with what I have to say. Is that a wolf sleeping under my desk or a relative of yours, Mike?"

"You're easily distracted, aren't you?" Sofia asked.

He pushed hair out of his face. "I haven't slept in days, and I'm down a couple of quarts. Deprivation definitely affects me."

"What information, Laurent?" Mike demanded. "Where's Cathy?"

"I don't know."

Mike took an angry step forward. "You don—"

"Let me finish. I believe Cathy's disappearance is part of a much bigger plan." He paused for a moment for dramatic effect. "There's a werewolf revolution afoot."

"I know," Mike said.

Laurent lost some of his bright enthusiasm. "What do you mean, you know?"

"Never mind how he knows," Sid said. "Tell us what you found out."

"I found out that local illegal arms dealers have been doing a lot of business with some hard-core biker types in the last few days. I've convinced one of them to let us do a ride-along on a delivery."

"You used telepathy on this man?" David Berus asked.

Laurent gave Berus an incredulous look. "Hell, no, I bribed him."

Jason liked this Laurent. When Berus threw back his head and laughed, Jason decided he liked him as well.

Sofia was not amused. "How is this going to help us find my cousin?"

"The bikers are holed up in a warehouse," Laurent answered. "We find the warehouse, we find Cathy."

Sid's phone rang before anyone could ask more questions.

"Hello, Harry. I'm going to put you on speakerphone so everyone can hear."

"We had the scent of a couple of the Hunyara family," Harry Bleythin said, "but their trail disappeared. Then we picked up a faint whiff, followed that, then it was gone again. I remembered how there was absolutely no trace of the feral at the motel when we were within a few feet of him. So I want to ask Mike if he has any information about how the feral managed that."

Mike said, "They've developed a chemical they spray on themselves that completely masks all scent. They must've used it on Cathy when they picked her up at her apartment."

"And now I suspect they've used this chemical on the Hunyaras."

"Cathy's a Hunyara," Sofia reminded them. "They kidnapped her, tried to get me, and now they've abducted more of my family."

"That's my conclusion," Harry said. "But I think this lack of scent is finally starting to work against them—now that I know what not to sniff for."

"I'm having a brilliant idea," Laurent spoke up.

"You usually do," Harry said. "What is it?"

"We come at them from both angles." He quickly filled Harry in on his information, then outlined his plan.

When Laurent was done, Harry said, "Roger that. We'll be in touch when we're in position."

"Count me in on this rescue," David Berus said.

"The more the merrier," Laurent said.

"I'm in," Antonia said.

Laurent, Sid, and Mike nodded without showing the least surprise, so Jason didn't think it was his place to protest the involvement of either female. They were Clan after all, and he was Family. Their customs were not his, although his own Matri would never permit a female to put herself in harm's way.

David spoke up. "Lady Antonia, is that wise?"

"I don't have to be wise," she answered with a gentle smile. "I'm a grown-up. I get to make up my own mind."

He put his hands on her shoulders. "But . . ."

They gazed into each other's eyes.

Everyone else looked on and forgot to breathe while the silence stretched out to eternity. The pair smiled at each other, and their expressions were identical, totally in harmony, totally content.

"I think I've been in mourning long enough," he said.

"So have I." Antonia put her hand on his cheek, and David turned his head to kiss her palm. It sealed a promise.

And broke the moment.

"I see where your daughter gets her independence," David said. "I like it."

Antonia chuckled. "It seems that you're going to have to get used to it."

"Mom?" Laurent and Sid asked.

So that's what the beginning of a bond looks like, Jason thought. *Beautiful.*

He wanted to pick up Sofia, whirl her around, and kiss her until they were both crazy with desire. He wanted to lay her down and give her all the pleasure she deserved. He wanted to hold her close to his heart and make promises and plans, and simply just be with her. But now was not the time.

"We'll get back to this later," David said. With his arm around her waist, he turned Antonia toward her gaping children. "Right now we've got a rescue to carry out."

Chapter Thirty-two

I can do this, Cathy thought. *I can transform.* She wanted to take a deep breath and close her eyes to relax, but a deep breath was out of the question with the chemical hanging in the air. It didn't help that they had cranked up the zapper device that blocked vampires' awareness of them. While the subaudible whine didn't cause her pain, it was distracting.

Cathy closed her eyes and stopped trying to concentrate. For over a year she'd been trying to learn how to be a werewolf. Maybe instinct was the key to what she needed to learn.

Go with the flow.

Flow. Yes, that was it. She brought up the memories of Walt changing from man to wolf and back again, and of all the times she'd seen the

Bleythin brothers do the same thing. She'd always assumed she had no control over the change, because she'd been told so. She had no doubt the natural-borns believed what they'd taught her, but she now chose to believe they were wrong.

Cathy slipped off her shoes and flexed her toes. She ran her awareness along the muscles of her calves and thighs. She blanked out how they felt now and superimposed the feel of wolf muscle stretching over her bones. She thought of her bones, and what shape they needed to take to support wolf muscle and sinew. She thought of fur, warm and soft, protecting her skin. And of skin tougher and more protective than human.

Flow, she thought. *Change. Be.*

"Cathy! No!"

She heard the shout just as her vision changed. Though her hearing grew more acute, she couldn't make out the word. She understood the fear in the sound and reacted with a snarl, revealing her long fangs. She was not afraid; she was alpha and would prove it.

She sprang toward the wall of the cage, but something held her back. Something was wrapped around her leg. It wouldn't budge when she tried to free her paw. She snapped. Her teeth came down on metal but couldn't break the restraint. She had to be free!

She didn't mind the pain.

The cage rattled; the door opened.

"They've got a zapper all right," Laurent said, putting a hand to his forehead and driving slower.

Beside him, Sid grimaced and squinted. The sunlight hurt her eyes. She glanced behind her to where the others sat. Daniel looked sympathetic and Sofia puzzled, but the three other vampires looked as uncomfortable as she felt. Having been briefed on the effects of the zapper, they didn't complain. "At least this proves we've got the right place," she told them.

A guard stepped in front of the SUV when they turned into the parking lot behind the warehouse. He held up a hand and showed a weapon.

Laurent stopped the van and rolled down the window. "I've got a delivery for you, friend."

The guard shook his head. "Not now."

Laurent gestured toward a wide metal door at the back of the building. Then he caught the man's gaze and said, "Open up. I'm not unloading out here."

If he was trying to psychically influence the werewolf, it didn't work.

"I said not now."

"They've got a situation inside," Daniel said

suddenly, his eyes closed. "Cathy's . . . bleeding."

"Go, Harry!" Laurent shouted into his cell phone as he stepped on the gas. He opened his door and it slammed into the guard as they passed. "Bloodsuckers out!"

Sid heard her brother shout, "Mortals duck!" as she jumped from her side of the vehicle. The other vampires went out the back door.

Dodging bullets as she ran, she managed to get the entrance to the warehouse open just as Laurent drove up to it.

With the van inside, Sid joined the other vampires in fighting the well-armed werewolves outside.

The van crashed into a truck parked inside the warehouse, and both car alarms began to whine. Laurent jumped out and Daniel scrambled after him.

After that, Laurent moved so quickly, Sofia could only make out a blur. She did hear him yell, "Ow! God damn it, silver bullets!"

A moment later a weapon landed on the floor and a body sailed through the air, screaming.

Daniel headed purposefully toward the far side of the warehouse and smashed a large machine.

It must have been the zapper, because Laurent

shouted, "Clear!" and the other vampires moved inside.

Bullets were still flying when Sofia cautiously slipped out of the van and searched the room for wolf shapes.

She ignored the trio of black beasts that came bounding inside; the Bleythins wouldn't be here if they hadn't taken care of the guards stationed outside.

Then she saw the cage and the man bending over something inside it. When he stood, she saw what she'd come looking for. Sofia started forward.

Before she'd gone two steps, the cream and gold werewolf pounced, pinning the man against the bars of the cage. And as he reached to push it away, the werewolf ripped open the man's throat.

Chapter Thirty-three

The smell of blood brought Sid to a momentary halt as she rushed inside, and she licked her lips. She sometimes forgot how spellbinding mortal blood could be. It permeated the soul, called up ancient hunger, tried to strip away the civilized veneer.

She pushed down the ancient part of herself and continued into the room, where Laurent was taking down one of the bad guys. There was blood on her brother's arm, his own.

"Eden's not going to like that," she called to him.

"I won't tell her if you won't," he called back. "It'll heal in a minute." He looked around. "All looks clear."

Daniel stepped around from the back of the

truck. "They're all down." He sighed. "Now we've got a crime scene to clean up."

Sid knew they wouldn't have much time; someone nearby was sure to report the sound of gunfire. The cops would be on the way soon.

Daniel took out his cell phone to call in the waiting cleanup team. Antonia came up to him and they began to consult in quiet tones. Laurent found the weapon that fired silver bullets and put it in the back of their van.

Sid heard a growl and turned to see a huge black body arcing through the air. Two other black werewolves stalked behind Mike, a fierce guard for the Tracker. Then she saw what the werewolves were headed toward: Cathy in wolf form, crouched over a human body. Her pale fur was stained with blood and her muzzle was buried in her victim's throat.

Her heart sank. "Oh, no," Sid whispered. "Stay back, Sofia," she said as the mortal moved forward.

But of course the woman didn't listen.

Sofia didn't want to go closer, but that was where she had to be, where she was needed. Her heart pounded hard and her head hurt.

"Cathy."

The beast looked up. It growled and tried to stare her down.

Sofia said, "No."

Then the Bleythin pack were there, and she automatically put herself between them and her cousin.

Mike changed into human shape in a quick blur. Behind Sofia, Cathy snarled.

"Get out of my way," he ordered.

"Leave her alone," Sofia replied. "Let me help her."

"There's no help for a killer feral. She dies right now."

"The hell she does!"

"You don't know our laws."

"You can't just put her down without knowing why—"

"She's moonchanged! That's why!"

"She's not," Jason said.

The calm in his voice soothed Sofia's anger; it seemed to have a similar effect on Mike.

Jason stood beside Cathy, his hand resting on top of her head. The beast shivered, but most of the insane fierceness had gone out of her eyes.

"You don't want to do this," Jason went on. "I've been inside your head, Mike. I know how much you love this woman."

"Shut up!" Mike shouted. He threw back his head and let out a rough-voiced howl that should never have come from a human throat.

Sofia finally realized that it wasn't fury driving the Tracker, but heartbreaking pain. Prepared to fight him, now she wanted to help him.

"The moon isn't full yet," she said. "We don't know why she changed, or how. We don't know why she killed." She pointed at the body. "He was her captor. What did he do to her? Was he a werewolf?"

Mike sniffed. "He was."

"Your world has changed," Jason said. "Your laws might not apply to this situation. If you act on instinct, you'll never forgive yourself."

"I can't think about myself. I can't do what *I* want."

Mike was stubborn, but Sofia sensed that his resolve was wavering. She said, "Cathy needs help. Please let me help her. There's a lot going on here. We need to find out what these bastards were up to. Let me get into Cathy's mind."

"She doesn't have a mind right—"

"We came here to rescue her," Sid said, stepping in front of Mike. "My vote is to take her home."

"I second Sid's vote," Laurent put in.

"This is werewolf business," Mike said.

"Your kin is affiliated with the Wolf Clan,"

Antonia pointed out. "We do not rule werewolf kind, but our Matri has some say in advising your kin. This is a complicated situation. I think you need Lady Juanita to mediate it."

Harry morphed into human and put a hand on Mike's shoulder. "They're right, bro. You know they are."

Mike stared at Cathy for a moment before his hard expression cracked into one of utter pain. "All right," he said. "Let's get her out of here."

Chapter Thirty-four

ou'll be all right?" Jason asked.

"I'll be all right," Sofia replied.

"You will be all right. I'm trying to reassure myself more than you, you know."

"I know. Trust me."

Jason sighed, brushed his lips across hers, then stepped back and closed the metal door. It was covered with gouges and scratch marks.

Sofia locked the door and looked around. The walls of the windowless room were thickly padded. She'd been told it was soundproofed as well. The room was in the rear of the Bleythin office building, and it was where Cathy was kept during the days she was in wolf form during the full moon.

The wolf Cathy was curled up in one corner.

Her head rested on her front paws and her eyes were half closed. Sofia was pretty sure Jason's mental influence was the reason Cathy wasn't currently raging around like a maniac.

"You look tired," Sofia told her. She stretched aching muscles. "I sure am."

Cathy had emptied large bowls of water and raw meat before lying down.

Sofia looked at the empty dishes and said, "You know, I can't remember when I ate last, or slept." She settled slowly onto the floor and leaned her back against the door. She kept her gaze on her cousin. "It's been a rough couple of days, hasn't it?"

Cathy lifted her head and showed a mouth full of fangs. A snarl rumbled low in her throat.

Sofia scratched her earlobe and fought off a yawn. "I'm too tired to be scared." Cathy's head dropped back to her paws. "You, too, huh? I'd like to be able to trust you not to attack, and leave you alone. Maybe with time you could figure the change out on your own. But your boyfriend is off consulting with his superiors, and I'm told that some vampire queen wants to have a talk with us. So, let's get to work proving that we Hunyara are a viable addition to the werewolf community."

She knew it was dangerous, but Sofia had to close her eyes to concentrate.

She heard Cathy move and shouted, *Stop!*

Cathy whimpered as Sofia invaded her mind. The action sent a wave of pain through both their heads, but Sofia didn't flinch away from what she had to do.

Cousin, we're going to make this up as we go along, but I promise you we're going to be okay.

If she was going to succeed, she couldn't doubt this for a moment herself.

"You have to trust her," Sid said. She pulled a chair up beside Jason's in the hall across from Cathy's room.

"I do trust her." He didn't look away from the door. "I also worry about her."

Sid took a seat and passed a steaming mug of coffee to Jason. He took a deep gulp. Only then did he look at her. She appreciated his blue eyes and sharp cheekbones, in an aesthetic way.

His eyes narrowed. "Just what are you thinking, daughter of the Wolf Clan?"

She took the mug out of his hand and took a drink. Jason's eyebrow shot up. She laughed. "I know sharing liquids has great symbolism among our kind, Prime of the Caegs, but mostly I wanted a hit of caffeine."

"Mostly?"

"It's complicated. Why is it that suddenly

everything to do with werefolk is complicated?"

"What the werefolk didn't know about for several generations hasn't done them any harm," he said. "No, that isn't true. The Hunyaras and the mortals trying to use them have been a ticking bomb. But I think your concern is very personal—and not just because Cathy Carter is your friend. You're not here to sit vigil, are you?"

She'd been bearing this secret alone for several years. She didn't want to be alone with it anymore. Besides, if anyone deserved an explanation for what she was about to ask, it was Jason Cage. There wasn't a Bleythin in the building, and Laurent had gone home to his wife and child. Sid felt safe enough to talk.

"No," she answered him. "I have been looking for an opportunity to talk to you alone. I think you're the only one in our world who could understand." His eyebrow canted questioningly once again. "I know what you did back in the forties, and why, and I don't think you were wrong."

Pain and regret flashed in his eyes. "I intruded into a mortal's mind and made him do things against his will. How is anything I did right?"

"You were trying to serve the greater good. To help mortals you loved."

He waved her words away. "Excuses."

"Reasons. Good ones." Sid took a deep breath

and plunged on. "I would have done the same. I have done the same."

She waited for his reaction, but all Jason Cage did was look at her and wait.

Sid put the mug on the floor and twisted her hands together in her lap. She hated the guilt and nervousness coursing through her. She was a person who worked hard to get what she wanted, for Goddess's sake! She was strong, independent. She shouldn't feel like a child in need of comfort and absolution.

"It's a long story," she said. "I need your promise to keep it to yourself."

"I'm not a Clan Prime," he reminded her. "It's not up to me to judge you. You have my silence," he added. "You're in love with a werewolf, aren't you?" he asked before she could blurt it out. "Which one? Harry?"

"Of course not! Harry's happily married to a mortal—a vet, actually. And please, no jokes about having a doctor in the family, because we've made them all already. I'm babbling, aren't I?"

"Yes. Young Joe Bleythin, then."

Sid closed her eyes until she got the naked longing under control. "Yes."

She'd just admitted to falling in love with a male who was not a Prime. It was the most dangerous thing a vampire female could do, and she waited with her breath held to see how the Prime would take it.

"You could get him killed."

She let out her breath. "I know." The fear gnawed at her every day. "He doesn't know. He's never going to know. I've seen to that, for his own good."

Jason's hands landed hard on her shoulders and he brought them both to their feet. "What have you done?"

His urgency ripped into her. "I—"

"Is there a bond between you? Is that possible?"

"No!" Not exactly. Some things were too private, too dangerous to share. "I messed with his mind, that's all." She gave a bitter laugh. "That's bad enough, even though I did it for his safety. When I realized how attracted we were to each other, I knew it had to be stopped. Werewolves disapprove of their people mating with mortals, though they don't outright forbid it. Harry's been ostracized by just about everyone but his brothers since he married Marj. I don't want Joe to have to choose between his people and me. Besides—"

"Your Clan Primes would kill him if he dared to touch you."

"Yes." She felt the familiar wave of dread for

Joe's safety. "At least, they'd kill him if they knew I wasn't interested in mating with anyone else."

"And you would lose your freedom if they found out about this love."

"Whatever I feel, I keep to myself," she told him. "I've made Joe believe that neither of us can be interested in being more than friends, that our species are too different to be attracted. I psychically brainwashed him, going against what the Clans stand for, but I did it for the right reasons."

"That was my defense six decades ago, and they put me in prison anyway. Of course, I was also sixteen and stupid. You're neither. Why are you *really* telling me about this?"

Chapter Thirty-five

Sofia continued thrusting her consciousness into her cousin's trapped mind.

Talk to me. Come on, I know you're in here somewhere. I'm getting tired of telepathically stomping around in a head filled with insanity and vicious cravings. I refuse to believe you really prefer dripping entrails to chocolate cheesecake.

Stop snarling at me, Catherine Sigornie Carter, or you'll have to put up with my rant about Great Expectations *again. Even worse, I'll start dissecting* The DaVinci Code. *When I posted about it on my blog, we argued about it for a month. Come on—wake up and argue with me again. Help me find your brain. Once you find your brain, you can find your way back to your human body. You made yourself into a wolf. Now take the next step—come back to yourself. Come back to me.*

All right, I'm going to say it, even if I really don't like the guy—come back to Mike. Come back for Mike. The two of you need to have a long talk. Maybe what you need is a good fight. Or to screw. But you can't do anything with him until you show him you're just as much a werewolf as he is. He may be the Tracker, but you're Hunyara, and that's just as good. Maybe even better. Definitely better. He doesn't deserve you.

Does . . .

You said something! Sofia responded to the faint, faraway whispered word. *Thank God! Do you know how sick I am of hearing my own voice, even if it is all in your head? Say something else.*

Sofia was answered by the usual snarl and growl from the beast dominating Cathy's mind. Well, if you have a weapon, use it.

Mike sucks, Sofia stated.

Does not, Cathy countered, the thought faint but adamant from behind the beast's fury.

Cathy, come back, Sofia called. *Come back . . .*

To Mike? For Mike?

A faint trace of hope reached Sofia.

For you. You have to do it for you. Face Mike as an equal. Love him as all you are.

"Good point," Cathy said with a human voice, a human woman once more.

Sofia sighed in utter weariness. Her shoulders rested against the padded wall, and Cathy's head rested heavily on her shoulder. It took all of Sofia's energy to raise her hand and stroke her cousin's cheek, which was wet with tears. Sofia realized that her cheeks were wet, as well. Tears, or sweat?

"I'm human," Cathy said. "How did you do that?"

"We did it together. From now on, you can do it on your own. Right?"

"Yeah," Cathy said after a long pause. "I think I can."

"Good. I need to sleep now."

"Me, too. Does your head hurt, too?"

"God, yes."

"Try meditating."

Sofia thought a bottle of aspirin might work better, but she didn't have the strength to move. "How does one meditate?"

"Open your mind," Cathy said. "Don't think."

That sounded easy enough. Go blank. Go to silence.

Jason . . .

Jason dreaded whatever was coming, but he

had to ask, "Why are you really telling me about this?"

"I owe my Clan children," Sid answered. "My Matri wanted me to have a child with David Berus, but I wasn't interested. Imagine my relief when he and my mother hooked up."

He knew Sidonie Wolf was different than other vampire females, but her attitude shocked him deeply. "You don't want to have children?"

"Of course I do!"

Her outrage pleased him. "But—"

"I accept my duty to my Clan and to my species. More than that, I very much look forward to being a mother. But I have a very big problem when it comes to the biological mechanism required for getting pregnant."

"You're infertile?"

"No. I simply can't bear the thought of having sex with a Prime. It would be wrong."

"So you're bonded to Joe."

"Only a little, and that's not the point. It's really very simple," Sid said. "I want you to father my child."

"But—you said you couldn't have sex with a Prime. I'm a Prime."

"Sex is not necessary for what I have in mind."

Chapter Thirty-six

The door across the hall flew open before Jason could say another word. He didn't know how to react to Sid's outrageous proposal, anyway.

"Jason?"

Sofia staggered out into the hall and he forgot all about Sid, scooping Sofia up in his arms. He kissed her forehead, then gently touched his lips to hers.

"You look terrible," he told her.

Her arms came around his neck. "I smell, too."

"I wasn't going to mention that. Come on, sweetheart, let me take you away from all this."

"Somewhere with a bed, I hope."

"Excuse me." Sid eased past them and went

into Cathy's den. Jason ignored the look she gave him before she closed the door.

The mattress was wonderfully comfortable. The sheets were smooth and soft, and smelled of vanilla and lavender. The blanket felt like velvet. She had to be dreaming, because this couldn't be the bed in her motel room. A warm body lay along the length of her back and thighs, making her feel safe and comforted. She'd had lots of dreams. The shadows of dark and fantastical images still spun inside her brain, but all was well while they were side by side.

Sofia sighed and came fully awake. She didn't recognize the room when she opened her eyes, but she'd never been anywhere so luxurious before.

"Jason?"

When she sat up and looked at the body beside her, she was disappointed to discover that George and Gracie were the ones keeping her company in the king-size bed.

"Jason?" she called again, and heard the sound of running water from a nearby bathroom. Naked, she got up and padded through the ankle-deep carpet toward the bathroom door.

The door opened before she reached it and Jason stood there wearing a plush black robe. He looked good in black, and she liked the way the robe gapped open to show his ripped chest and abdomen.

"Hello, beautiful," he said.

She was too aware of aches and pains all over to feel beautiful, but her body still reacted to his burning gaze. Heat flooded her insides and her nipples stiffened. He stepped forward to brush his thumbs across the hard peaks.

"What you do to me," she murmured.

"Just wait," Jason said. Then he glanced over her shoulder. "Excuse me." He crossed the room and opened a patio door that faced a courtyard garden. "Out," he ordered the wolves. "And don't do anything to embarrass me," he added as the animals ran outside. Jason closed the door and drew a curtain across it. "Alone at last," he said, turning back to her.

"Where are we?" she asked. "And how'd we get here? Vampire magic?"

"I drove," he said. "You fell asleep on the way over."

She blinked. "Yeah. I sort of remember that."

"We are guests of Lady Juanita at the Citadel of the Wolf Clan. Actually, it's a mansion in La Jolla."

"Lady Juanita's the vampire queen?"

"Not mine," he answered. "She's the head of the Wolf Clan. I'm a Family Prime. She isn't my Matri, but I do have to defer to her in her territory."

Sofia listened to this and rubbed her forehead. "I guess I have a lot to learn about vampire and werewolf social structures."

"You'll have a chance to learn this evening. We've been invited to the Council of Elrond after supper."

"The book or movie version?" she asked. "The council is actually my favorite part of *The Lord of the Rings*."

"Mine, too," he answered. "I was never fond of Tolkien's antitechnology stance, but I love his world-building and the history and mythology—"

"Keep talking sexy to me like that, and I'm going to throw you on the bed and have my way with you." She grinned.

"I'm all in favor of ravishing and being ravished." Jason gestured toward the bathroom. "But first I've run you a hot bath."

She sighed gratefully. "I can certainly use one."

Jason took her hand and led her into the huge bathroom, which was bigger than her entire apartment. It was all pale marble and glass bricks, highlighted with indirectly lit mirrors and matte chrome, and furnished with stacks of thick, royal blue towels.

She stared at the bathtub. "Does this thing come with a lifeguard?"

"I'm your lifeguard." He lifted her and eased her into the wonderful warm water. She leaned her head back against the marble rim and watched appreciatively as Jason shed his robe. What a magnificent body the man had!

"Yes, I'm hot," he said with an ironic smile. When he climbed into the water with her he added, "It's a wonder it doesn't sizzle and steam."

Sofia held her arms out to him. "I think I'm in charge of doing that." But even as he came close and their lips touched, her concerns began to surface.

Take this time for yourself, he whispered in her mind. *For us.* His hands moved through the water and over her.

His thoughts eased her and his touch stimulated; the combination sent her into a blissful haze. "I can't remember how many days it's been since we met," she said.

"Does it matter?" he asked.

His mouth came down on hers and nothing mattered but sensation for a long time after that. At some point her tongue brushed across the sharp points of his teeth, and they shared the heady taste of a drop of blood.

He drew away from her then, even though she whimpered and tried to pull him back.

He chuckled and said, "I like you this way, Wolf Tamer, all needy and hungry." She bared her teeth and Jason laughed. He picked up a sponge and a bottle of bath gel. "Lean back and relax. If I can bathe tigers, I think I can manage one grubby wolf tamer."

"Grubby?" She splashed water at him, even though it was true. "How hard can it be to give tigers a bath? They like water."

"But they don't like soap."

"I like both."

She relaxed in the deep, warm water as Jason's deft hands worked magic on her with sensual touches and creamy, flower-scented lather from her toes to the top of her head. His fingers skimmed along her skin and kneaded away all the soreness in her muscles. His gentle care both soothed and stimulated. When his fingers moved between her thighs, and then inside her, she shuddered with an orgasm at this first intimate touch.

He kissed her throat, nibbled on her ear, and whispered, "If I make love to you now, I'll just have to wash you all over again."

She pressed against him. "I can live with that." She closed her hand around the cock pressing against her belly, stroked the length of it, then guided him inside her. She wrapped her legs around his hips in the buoyant water and he positioned her against the side of the tub.

He made love to her then in long, slow strokes that took her up and over the edge many times, before he joined her in a final explosive orgasm.

Chapter Thirty-seven

When she first stepped into the courtyard and saw Mike playing with the wolves, Cathy paused and smiled. He was a pain in the ass, but she couldn't help but like the big man when she caught him not acting all dour and dangerous.

The moment didn't last long, of course. He sensed her presence and waved the animals away. Turning a frown on her, he said, "You shouldn't be here."

"We're living under vampire rules right now." She snorted. "I now understand what you meant when you said being around vampires plugs up your psychic nose. I don't exactly have a headache, but I don't exactly not have one, either. And our hosts won't let me see my cousin. I was informed that 'the bonding pair needs privacy'—as if we don't have more important things to deal with than Sofia's sex life! Since I couldn't see her, I decided to work things out with you."

"We have nothing to work out." His look dared her to approach.

She took the dare.

The wolves, being sensible creatures, slunk away from a confrontation of two werewolves.

When they were standing toe to toe in front of the garden's central fountain, Cathy pointed up at the clear blue sky. "There's a full moon hidden up there," she told him. "You will note that I'm not wearing a fur coat."

He said nothing.

"Come with me," she said.

She turned around and walked to the entrance of the room she'd been given. She knew he tried hard not to follow her, to be stern and unbending. She also didn't doubt for a moment that he would give in. When he grudgingly came inside, she closed the patio door and drew the curtains.

"Now that we're alone . . ." Cathy pulled her dress over her head. She wasn't wearing anything underneath.

Mike stared.

He was looking at her as a man, which pleased her, but that wasn't what she aimed for at the moment.

"I've been practicing this all day," she told him, and changed into a wolf.

Mike tensed as though he expected her to attack. It took all of her newfound control not to snarl at the insult. She took a step back and sat, carefully not looking into his eyes. She wasn't here to play dominance games, at least not of the traditional kind. She didn't want to be more alpha than Mike Bleythin.

"I'm trying to prove a point," she told him when she turned back to human, and he continued to stare.

"Prove whatever it is to the council," he answered, his voice rough.

"Don't you want to know?"

"It won't matter."

She wanted to grow claws and rake them across the stubborn fool's chest. But full moon or not, she was in control of her volatile werewolf emotions. She stomped one bare foot into the thick carpet to vent her frustration. "This is between you and me, and it matters."

"There isn't anything betw—"

"Then why are you looking at me like that?"

"You're gorgeous, and you're naked. What else am I supposed to do?"

She put her hands on her hips and thrust her breasts out. "You could make love to me. It's all

I've wanted since the day we met. You've never told me you love me or that you even care, but I know you do."

"I can't," he said. "I won't."

He started to turn toward the door but Cathy grabbed his hand and pulled him closer. He gasped as their thighs brushed together.

"It's just lust," he said. "Ordinary, healthy lust. It doesn't mean anything."

"It could. It will. We can be together now, Mike." His eyes closed when she pressed her body against his. "I feel how hard you are. I can smell how much you want me. Stop fighting what you want, what you need. You're a lonely man, Michael Bleythin, but I'm here for you."

"I'm not a man," he ground out. "And you're a feral." His hands grasped her shoulders; she could feel them shaking. "I will not mate with someone I may have to kill."

"You won't have to kill me."

"Are you trying to seduce me to go against the council?"

"Oh, screw the council! This is about *you*. I know you, and I know exactly what will happen if you kill me."

"What?"

"The guilt and grief will drive you crazy. And when you go crazy, you fall off the wagon.

There's nothing more dangerous than a drunken werewolf. This time, you won't make it into rehab—you'll go feral. Then your poor brothers will have to hunt you down and kill you. Since I am very fond of your brothers, I intend to spare them that."

"How kind."

"Not to mention the fact that I have too much to do to let you kill me." She grinned. "Oh, yeah— and I love you."

He stroked the back of his hand across her cheek. She grabbed it and kissed his palm, then placed his hand on her breast.

"Woman . . ." he growled.

"Mate," she answered. "I'm no feral. I'm no danger to werefolk. I am what you want and who you need, and it's time you faced up to it and took me to bed."

She put her hand behind his head and brought his mouth down to hers. The kiss they shared was eager, fierce, and hungry, just the way it should be between alpha mates.

I love you, I love you, I love you, he told her.

I know.

He drew away to look at her. "What about the council? What about what happened to you? What about your fam—"

"Later." She began to unbutton his shirt. "I'll

explain everything and take care of the council later. Right now, let us take care of each other."

All the fight went out of him; only the desire remained. "All right."

Cathy whooped with joy when he finally picked her up and carried her to the bed.

Chapter Thirty-eight

$\mathcal{S}$ofia smiled at herself in the mirror as she brushed out her damp curls.

"You look like a cat that's been into the cream," Jason said.

He stood framed by the doorway, once again dressed in the black plush robe. She had a huge towel wrapped around her.

"I feel like one, too." Their gazes met in the glass, making her tingle inside and out all over again.

"Speaking of cream," he went on. "Are you hungry?"

"Yes," she answered promptly. "In more ways than one, and you know it."

He grinned. "Me, too. But I was thinking of breakfast right now." He glanced into the bedroom. "And some very kind person has left us a tray of goodies. Do you by any chance like baklava?"

"Baklava," she said eagerly, and abandoned her hair without another thought.

"I see you can be seduced by honey and rose-water."

She smiled at him. "Dip yourself in honey sometime and see what happens."

"I'll do that."

The tray of food sat on a small table near the patio doors. She surveyed the selection of pastries, glasses of orange juice, and a carafe of coffee, and rubbed her hands together in delight. "I like vampire room service."

Jason held out a chair for her before taking the chair on the other side of the table. "A peaceful citadel does have a five-star-hotel quality to it." He gestured toward another door. "In there will be a closet full of clothes in many styles and sizes. A Matri never knows who is going to drop in, why, or for how long, so she prepares for all sorts of guests. We're trained quite strictly as children that courtesy and hospitality are part of the glue that holds a civilized culture together."

"Why 'quite strictly'?"

"Because vampire babies are spoiled rotten

little savages." He poured her a cup of coffee. At the same time he ran a bare foot up the length of her calf.

She clasped the fine china cup in her hands as a shiver of desire ran through her. Sofia gave Jason a firm look. "Breakfast first. Then I intend to have my way with you."

"Eat faster," he suggested. He glanced at her throat and his lips uncovered fangs. "But eat a lot. I need you to keep up your strength."

She stuck her tongue out, far more turned on than daunted by the idea of a vampire longing to taste her. Her insides tightened and her nipples hardened at the very thought of it.

Everything was fresh and delicious. The texture of the delicate china dishes alone made her feel like she was going to be caught out at any moment and sent to the kitchen to do the dishes.

"Think of yourself as a lost princess who's been found," Jason said, catching her thoughts.

"The luxury is almost overwhelming," she said as she looked around.

"As children, we are also taught to invest wisely. If you're going to live a long time, it's best to live well."

That made a great deal of sense. Then again, she was so attracted to this man that just about anything he did or said was fine with her. She stood, let the towel drop to a blue puddle around her feet, and held out her hand.

He took it without a word and followed her to the bed, where she took off his robe and they lay down together.

Then he made her feel like far more than a princess. He made her feel like a goddess, worshipped, adored, and satisfied.

"Satiated?" he asked after he'd brought her to orgasm more times than she could count.

Sofia gazed up at the ceiling and let out a long breath. "Hell, no," she answered.

Jason rolled onto his side and patted her hip. "That's what I like to hear."

She looked at him through half-closed eyes. "Though I think I've had more sex today than in all the rest of my life combined." She yawned and stroked a hand up his thigh. "I bet the same cannot be said for you."

Jason gave an unapologetic shrug. "Sex with you makes me forget every other time, place, and person."

Sofia was willing to go with that romantic explanation. A memory of the conversation she'd overheard between Jason and Sid Wolf returned—but she might well have dreamed that, so she let it go.

Jason pulled the sheet up over her. "Excuse me a moment."

He got up and opened the patio door. The wolves came bounding in and jumped up on the end of the bed. Sofia considered shooing them off, but decided it wasn't worth the effort. How her world had changed. She not only had a family and a purpose and a lover, but not very long ago she hated and feared every canine in the world. Now she was becoming fond of George and Gracie.

"Remember that they aren't pets," Jason said, getting back into bed beside her.

She turned to face him. "What are they, then?"

"Friends." He glanced at the animals and smiled. "A reminder."

There was sadness in his words, a hint of loneliness and old pain in his eyes. Sofia began to suspect why wolves were so important to Jason Cage, and she moved closer to him. His arm came around her shoulders.

Sofia rested against him for a while, basking in the heat of his body and the masculine scent of him. It would kill her if she had to leave him. *Take this time for yourself,* he had said. *For us.*

"It's good to just *be* together," Jason said.

Sofia was certain that he hadn't read her thoughts, yet he seemed to know her, body, mind, and soul. There were too many things about him she didn't know.

"Are some things too painful to talk about?" she asked.

"Yes. But that doesn't mean you don't have the right to know about me. All you have to do is ask."

Awed by Jason's emotional generosity, Sofia almost remained silent, but curiosity finally got the better of her. "What's it like? Being in a vampire prison?"

He gave her a gentle, lingering kiss, letting her know that lack of physical contact had been a devastating part of his punishment.

"They took my name from me," he said, then brushed his lips across hers again. "Belonging to our Family, our Clan, or our Tribe is very important to us. Exile can be permanent, but my Family took me back after I'd learned my lesson. I spent much of my time alone. It nearly drove me crazy."

"You are the farthest thing from crazy that I've ever met."

He caressed her cheek. "Thank you, even if you didn't think so at first."

"Having learned that every crazy thing is true, I now know that I'm nuts and you're the lucid one."

"But you didn't know me in my youth, not after the glimpses of the past I've shown you. Maybe if you'd been born all those decades ago, I would have found you when I first went hunting."

"Hunting for what?"

"I don't know if it was something my guards allowed me to do, or something I got away with. But when I couldn't take solitary confinement anymore, I sent my spirit out of my body. My people are all telepathic, but I've always been more psychic than most. Though I couldn't physically leave my prison, I learned how to psychically be free—at least for a little while. I think the mortal term for what I did is astral projection. To me it was my only means of escape. I'd learned my lesson and stayed away from mortal minds, but I'd always been comfortable with wolves, so I telepathically found the pack I used to play with as a child and ran with them whenever I could. I became a wolf. It was very good for me: I learned a great deal about cooperation and leadership; when to run and hide and when to stand and fight." He looked at George and Gracie. "I owe the wolves a lot."

Sofia rolled over to lean on his chest and look down at him. "So I guess running with the wolves helped you learn how to tame the Wolf Tamer."

A sly smile lifted his lips. "Are you tame?"

"Want to find out?" she asked, and straddled his hips.

She leaned forward to kiss him, and his hands cupped her breasts.

But a knock sounded on the door before they could do anything else. "Excuse me," a voice called. "But you have half an hour until dinner."

Resisting the urge to scream in frustration, Sofia called back, "Thank you."

Jason continued to caress her breasts. "Do you think half an hour's enough time?" he asked with a wicked smile.

She smiled back as she positioned herself over his erection. "Let's find out."

Chapter Thirty-nine

"I've never seen a more beautiful night." Sofia lowered her gaze from the magnificent full moon to Jason's face, which she found even more magnificent.

"Neither have I," he said. "And I've seen a lot of nights."

"I could howl at a moon like that."

"The werewolves might think it rude," he warned. "I'd prefer laying you down in the jasmine and making love to you."

"I'd like that, too. Though I still might howl with passion if we did."

He sighed. "If only we had time to find out."

They were standing in the courtyard garden with their arms around each other's waist. Dinner was over and they were waiting to be called inside to the meeting. The air was scented with night-blooming flowers, and the murmur of the central fountain added its soothing sound. Peace permeated her senses out here.

"You see this differently than I do, don't you?" she asked the vampire. "This place is arranged to be at its best in the dark."

"Yes," he said. "Lady Juanita doesn't take the daylight drugs, so darkness is her world."

"Why not?" Sofia asked.

She dreaded the upcoming meeting with werewolves and vampires, with the Four Horsemen of the Apocalypse playing bridge in the corner, for all she knew. She welcomed any knowledge she could get and appreciated any distraction.

Dinner had been friendly enough. Their hostess had been gracious, everyone had flirted with everyone, there had been no serious conversation. She'd been able to tell which ones were werewolves, but she still couldn't tell the differences between vampires and mortals. Everyone had seemed normal. Almost everyone present had been wearing black, but since she'd picked a black dress out of a multicolored selection in the closet for herself, she couldn't even count that as odd.

"At dinner," she said, "I kept expecting unicorns or house elves to show up to clear the dishes."

"Were you disappointed? Maybe Lady Juanita's chef is named Igor. Shall we ask?"

"No. But do you know why she doesn't take medicine so she can go out in the daylight? Is she allergic?"

"Some of us are allergic," Jason said. "But taking the drugs is a personal choice. Lady Juanita believes in living a natural, unenhanced life. She doesn't forbid the rest of her Clan from benefiting from modern science, but she doesn't encourage it, either. Since we don't know the long-term effects of—"

"Excuse me, but you are wanted inside now," a young man said, stepping silently out of the darkness. He gave Sofia a quick once-over and an inviting smile, and disappeared just as quickly.

"That," she said, "was a vampire. I'm beginning to be able to tell the boys, at least, because you're all horny all the time."

Jason took her hand to lead her inside. "We're called Primes," he reminded her. "And you are absolutely correct."

"This is not going to be pleasant," Mike whispered as they took their seats on a leather sofa in the large central room. There were no windows and only one door, with Clan Primes standing guard on either side.

"Scared?" Cathy asked. She took it as a good sign that he sat beside her. It was a bad sign that every werewolf in the room glared at him when he did so.

She twined her fingers with his as he gave her a nod.

Sofia and Jason Cage were the last people to enter. Once they were inside, the door was closed and the Prime guards moved to stand in front of it.

"I guess no one's leaving until the vampires say so," Cathy whispered to Mike.

"You know how they always like being in charge," he whispered back. "And I'm not sure that's a bad thing right now. I might have killed you if they hadn't interfered."

"We've talked that through already. Just don't try it again."

He patted her on the knee. "Yes, dear."

Sofia and Cage joined them on the sofa, and Cathy wondered, *Now what?* as the stares from every point in the room grew even more fierce.

"I welcome all of you to my citadel," Lady Juanita said, drawing everyone's attention. "First, Jason, will you please explain what you know about the Hunyara to everyone."

Cathy was deeply interested in this. "Yeah, Jason, Mom never told me anything."

"Wait for it," Sofia whispered. "It's like going to a movie, only—"

"Ladies, please," Jason said. "Since I can't touch everyone in the room, I must concentrate very carefully to communicate telepathically to all of you."

Chapter Forty

Cathy found out what Jason meant as his memories of everything he knew about her mother's family filled her mind. Everything she found out tallied with what she'd learned from Eric.

When Jason was done, Cathy stood up. "My turn," she said.

She explained about how she'd been captured and what her captors wanted from her. She didn't tell them everything, since there were people who needed to be rescued, and she wasn't sure if the werefolk would want to help or destroy the Hunyara. There was certainly plenty of hostility from the werewolves as they listened.

"The people who took me are a threat to all of us," she continued. "They aren't just a gang of crazed feral werewolves. They're organized, fanatical, well funded, and high-tech. They want to destroy werefolk and vampires and anyone else who stands in their way. They have their own agenda, but I have the impression that they're working with allies. Supernatural kind has enemies, but we Hunyara aren't among them.

"There's a full moon tonight, and as a mortal who suffered a werewolf attack, I should be howling at that moon right now. Everyone knows that bitten werewolves turn into mindless monsters during the full moon.

"Thanks to Sofia Hunyara's wolf-taming gift, I've learned to control the madness. I am now no different than any natural-born."

Her claim was greeted with hostile silence. Maybe she shouldn't have put it quite like that, but damn it, it was true!

"What is the matter with you people?" she demanded. "The Hunyara aren't the problem."

"Tracker," one of the werewolf elders finally said. "Why is this creature still alive? It admits to being feral, but you do nothing."

"Even worse," another werewolf said, "you have shielded a feral and protected it. You of all—"

"What a bunch of jerks," Sofia interrupted.

"Destroy the feral!" the elder shouted at Mike.

"The hell I will!" He sprang to his feet and

looked around, challenging all the others. Most looked away. "Our world has changed, and I'm not your damn Tracker anymore."

"Haven't you listened to a word Cathy's said?" Sid spoke into the sudden shocked silence. The vampire female walked out of a shadowed corner of the room to stand beside Cathy and Mike. She glanced toward Lady Juanita. "With your permission?"

"Say what you wish," the Matri answered. "The opinions of all are welcome."

Sid knew very well that the werefolk resented her interference, but no one was going to argue with the Matri.

"I respect werefolk," Sid said. "I work with the Bleythin pack and count them as my friends."

She forced herself to remain calm and reasonable in the face of building animosity. She even sensed Joe's anger at her.

"I am an outsider to the pack structure, but because I am a vampire of the Wolf Clan, which is affiliated with werewolves, I've observed and studied werewolves my entire life. I know that while vampires and werewolves are longtime allies, our methods of coping and dealing with the mortal world have taken drastically different directions in the last century. We agree that hiding from mortals is the safest means of protecting ourselves. Vampires have turned to science and technology as a means to hide in plain sight. Werefolk have taken a very different road. I think that it is a narrow, dangerous road that will lead to your extinction."

"Ain't that the truth," Harry chimed in.

"Traitor!" a female elder snarled at him.

"I've never done anything against the laws of our kind," Harry pointed out. "Marrying a mortal is not forbidden."

"It should be," the elder shot back.

"Why?" a white-haired representative of the werefolk chimed in.

"Continue, Sidonie of House Antonia," Lady Juanita commanded.

"Werefolk have hidden so long and so deeply that I don't think even they know what they're hiding from anymore. You don't allow werefolk to change their mortal lovers; you even discourage them from having mortal lovers. When mortals do somehow get bitten, you don't allow the bitten mortals into your packs, even though the natural-born birthrate gets lower every generation—"

"The bitten can never be trusted!" an elder proclaimed.

"They're abominations," said another.

"Bullshit!" Cathy yelled.

"History shows that bitten werefolk can learn

to be calm during the moonchange given time," Sid went on.

"It isn't the *law* to kill the bitten just because a feral attacked them," Mike pointed out. "But it has become the custom. A custom that I've been expected to carry out. I've become sick of killing people who were victims themselves, and you're angry with me because I stopped doing it."

"Your council has decreed the destruction of all ferals, even the ones that could be tamed," Sid said. "But you can use the Hunyara to—"

"We have to protect ourselves," an elder interrupted. "These Hunyara are outsiders." The elder pointed at her. "You're an outsider. Vampires have no business interfering in our dealings with these Hunyara."

"I think you might be wrong about that," Cathy spoke up.

She turned to Lady Juanita. "My captor told me something that I didn't believe at the time, but the more I think about it, the more sense it makes. He told me that the Hunyara are descended from an offspring of a vampire and a werewolf."

"That's not possible," Joe declared.

"We don't know that," Juanita answered. "Continue."

Cathy noted that the vampires looked as stunned at this revelation as the werefolk. They didn't look as offended, though. Primes, she concluded, would make it with anything that moved.

She gestured at Sofia, who stood and looked around. There was telepathic power in that look that registered on every psychic in the room. None of the werefolk could meet her gaze for more than a few seconds.

Cathy let out a long breath and rubbed her forehead. "Werewolves can't do what she just did, but vampires can. She used the understanding of werewolf instincts and the psychic power of a vampire to save me."

"Maybe the Hunyaras are a cross between the best of both our kinds," Sid said, taking up Cathy's argument. "We need to study them to find out how their gift works. More important, the werefolk need to start thinking like they live in the twenty-first century and let the Hunyara use their gift for the good of all of us. In the meantime, I request that the Matri of the Wolf Clan grant the Hunyara protection."

This sent the werefolk into a frenzy of argument. Cathy, Sid, and Sofia looked at one another and silently agreed to stay out of it. Jason and Mike stood protectively next to them.

"Nothing's getting resolved," Sofia whispered.

"I know," Sid replied. "But we've made a beginning. There's so much that has to be brought out into the open, it's going to take a long time to settle."

"In the meantime, we've got more pressing matters to deal with," Cathy said.

"What aren't you telling us?" Jason asked.

"That most of the bad guys got away with Hunyara hostages."

Sofia swore; Mike roared. Suddenly everyone in the room looked their way. The psychic interference from the vampires as well as the others' shouting had kept their conversation quiet, but Lady Juanita wasn't the only one to give them shrewd, suspicious looks.

When the Matri spoke into the heavy silence, everyone paid attention. "Since there is clearly so much more we need to learn from these Romany, I grant all members of the Hunyara bloodline the protection of the Wolf Clan." She looked around, but nobody was stupid enough to argue. Her gaze settled on Jason. "Will my protection be enough to bring the Hunyara out of hiding?"

"I believe it will," Jason answered.

"But how—" Sofia began.

"It's the twenty-first century, remember?" He took out his cell phone. "I've got Uncle Pashta on speed dial."

Chapter Forty-one

Sofia didn't like it when the Matri took Jason off for a private chat after the meeting; being separated from Jason was almost physically painful for a few moments. Annoyed with herself for being so needy, she went outside in search of privacy, cutting through the garden on the way back to their room. She noticed Sid Wolf sitting on a bench by the fountain and started to pass by with only a nod of greeting.

But the vampire woman looked so forlorn, Sofia couldn't help but stop and ask, "What's the matter?"

She'd always made a point never to pry into other people's business and had avoided making friends, but a lot of her emotional barriers were melting away lately. As for never falling in love—well, she'd certainly screwed up that intention. Damn.

"You're scared," Sid answered. "Terror is coming off of you in waves." She patted the bench beside her, and Sofia took a seat.

"You don't look so happy yourself." She glanced around the garden. "Who are you hiding from?"

Sid sighed. "It's a long story."

"Sordid?"

"Completely. What are *you* scared of? You can't lose Jason, you know. That's what bonding's all about."

"But do I want to keep him? Or anyone? What if I have to spend my life defending the Hunyara from all those werefolk?" The prospect of battles to come made her doubt any possibility of settling down and living happily ever after.

"You might have to do that," Sid agreed. "But does doing your duty really have to interfere with you and Jason? Do you think he'll let it?"

"I don't know. No. But what about what I—"

"Mortals have free will, don't they?"

Sofia nodded.

"Primes do, too. You two will be fine."

Sofia didn't know if that was true, but she still found it reassuring. They sat in companionable silence for a few minutes. Sofia enjoyed the jasmine-scented evening breeze and the splashing of the fountain. "Do you live here?" she asked after a while.

"No. I've got my own place. That might change soon, though."

Sofia sensed that Sid didn't want to pursue that subject. She recalled Sid's part in the meeting and said, "You're quite the politician, aren't you? I was impressed by the way you worked the situation around so that the Matri offered to protect my family."

"That was more Cathy's doing than it was mine. She provided the vital information; I used it. I was raised to be a diplomat. I'd rather be a warrior, but I'm likely to end up being a Matri."

"Then watch out, world." Sofia grinned.

Sid gave her a conspiratorial smile. "Maybe. I need to have a few kids first, start my own house." She shook her head. "That's going to be complicated, but having children is important."

Sofia considered the vampire for a moment. "I like you, Sid," she said. "But I won't if you try to play me. Why don't you tell me straight up what you want?"

Sid smiled at her. "I'd hate to sit across a negotiation table from you."

"Isn't that what we're doing? Your conversation with Jason about wanting his baby wasn't something I dreamed, was it?"

Sid looked around as though frightened of being heard. *How much of this "dream" conversation do you remember?*

I want you to father my child. Sex is not necessary for what I have in mind, Sofia remembered. "You're looking for a sperm donor."

Sid nodded. Then she proceeded to telepathically whisper her reasoning into Sofia's head.

It gave Sofia a great deal to think about, but they were interrupted by Joe Bleythin's arrival before she could ask any questions.

"I've been looking for you, Sidonie."

He sounded calm, but the furious wolf Sofia sensed beneath the surface made her skin crawl.

Sid stood. "I thought you might be." She looked like she was prepared for the worst.

Sofia knew she didn't belong here. Dealing with this werewolf was Sid's business.

As she walked away, she heard Joe say, "Lucy, you got some 'splainin' to do."

"What can I say?" Sid asked. "I'm as surprised as you are."

"Do you know that you blink when you lie?"

"I do not!"

Joe gave a harsh laugh. The air around them seemed to grow colder. "So you are lying."

He knew her too well—except for the things

she'd made him forget. Sid turned away. "I do not want to have this conversation with you, Joseph Bleythin. At least not here and now."

"What *did* you know?" he demanded. "When did you know it, and for how long? And exactly what have you *not* been telling me?"

"About the Hunyaras? I don't know any more than you do about the bad guy's claims about Cathy's family." That was true, even if . . .

"Your species didn't seem repulsed by the idea of mating with members of my species when the subject came up. Why was I the one who protested?"

Sid shrugged. "Well, you know Primes . . ."

"How much have you lied to me? Why?"

His anger was shredding her. "It's complicated." She sighed. "Maybe the lesson should be to never do anything for anyone else's own good—because it'll only come back and bite you in the ass."

"Explain that to me."

"Okay." She looked up at the moon rather than at Joe, then took a deep breath. "I love you."

He was silent for a long time. She heard him pace around the fountain, then come back to her.

"I don't love you," he said.

Sid made herself look him in the eye. "Yes, you do. You just don't remember."

After that, the shouting started.

Chapter Forty-two

Sofia was surprised to find Jason already in their room when she reached it. He'd changed into black silk pajama bottoms, in which he looked mighty fine, and was lying on the bed reading a book. She instantly wanted to climb on beside him and toss aside the book.

"And you a lover of literature," he said, looking up and raking her with a hot gaze.

"Some things are more important than a good book." She chuckled. "That would be considered heresy if I posted it on my blog. Then again, it would be considered porn if I posted what I'm currently considering—and I'd get a lot more hits than I do talking about books."

He put the book on the nightstand and patted the mattress beside him. "Come here."

"Give me a minute."

She smiled and went into the walk-in closet. If he could wear black silk, so could she. She found a sexy, lacy confection in a lingerie drawer and quickly slipped into it. She gave a brief glance in the full-length mirror to check the effect, then shook out her long curls so that they rested on her shoulders and framed her face.

"How do I look?" she asked, stepping back into the bedroom.

He looked her over, eyes lighting with lust. "Wanton," was his response.

"What a lovely, old-fashioned word." She slinked forward, and he rose to meet her. "George and Gracie aren't likely to disturb us, are they?"

He took her in his arms. "They're kenneled up, and the evening is ours." He nuzzled her throat, kissed across her collarbone and down between her breasts.

Sofia curled her toes in the deep carpet. "That feels sooo nice." She ran her hands over his shoulders and arms, relishing the feel of sculpted muscles and warm flesh. "What did the Matri want with you?"

He gave her a look that said this wasn't the time or place for conversation, but after a moment he gave in to her curiosity. "She's concerned about Sidonie. She wanted to know if I knew any Prime among the Families that might spark Sid's interest."

"What did you tell her?"

"That I'd think about it."

"Um . . ."

Jason drew away from her. "What?"

"Can we talk? About Sid."

He looked almost panic-stricken. "I don't know what you overheard, but—"

"I know she wants to have your baby. Rather, she wants you to father her baby."

Jason sat down on the bed and stared at her. "You're taking this calmly."

He wasn't. The agitation that boiled off him made her head hurt.

"I begin to suspect a cultural problem here that I have no clue about." She pulled up a chair to sit down, rested her folded hands on the smooth silk of her nightgown, and kept her tone reasonable and as academic as she could manage. "Walk me through this, please. I have been given to understand that vampires are matrilineal." Jason nodded. "Women are heads of households, and all children belong to the mother and are part of the mother's Clan, no matter who the father is, whether they're bonded or not."

"That is correct."

"And it is not only customary, but necessary for the viability of the species, for vampire women to have children with several vampire males. They reproduce this way until they acquire a bondmate, and after the bonding they only have children with the Prime who is their bondmate."

"Yes."

"Okay, so, Sidonie is not bonded."

He gave her a hot look that made her shiver all over. "I am."

Sofia refused to give in to the strong urge to forget about everything and throw herself on the man. "You're working on being bonded. I believe the process of mind-soul-body integration takes some time."

"*We're* working on being bonded," he answered. "You and I. Sidonie Wolf has nothing to do with it."

"No, she doesn't. She doesn't want to have anything to do with you sexually. I'd cheerfully kill her if she did. She simply wants you to contribute your DNA to conceiving a child that will be totally hers. She wants to take the sex out of an ancient custom and put a modern spin on it. She wants a sperm donor—that's all."

"All?"

He stood, with grace that barely covered his outrage. For a moment Sofia shrank back in her chair. It was like having a furious giant standing over her, but she didn't give in to the intimidation for long. She met his gaze, Wolf Tamer to Beast Master, and after a few seconds of mutual glaring Jason resumed his seat. He hadn't calmed down at all, though. This was *so* not going well.

"I really don't understand why you're angry."

He crossed his arms over his bare chest. "You want to pimp me out to stud, and you wonder why I'm angry?"

"Oh, please. That's just male ego talking. I thought you were better than that."

"I am Prime!"

"Good for you," she snapped as her own temper flared. She shot to her feet and glared down at him this time. "Aren't you the person who recently pointed out that this is the twenty-first century? What's wrong with vampires using alternate fertility methods?"

"That's sick and disgusting and utterly—"

"Mortal?" she questioned sarcastically.

"Yes," he snarled back. "If Sid wants a baby, let her do it the right way—instead of using you to try to get to me."

It wasn't that she really wanted him to be Sid's

sperm donor, but she saw the other woman's point, and her desperation. "Jason, you're being old-fashioned."

"In this, yes. I belong to you." He grabbed her shoulders hard. "And you're mine. Conversation closed. Do you understand?"

Chapter Forty-three

Jason knew instantly that he hadn't phrased that right. He took his hands off her shoulders, terrified that he'd left bruises, and clasped his hands tightly behind his back. "I'm sorry. I—"

Sofia turned away from his apology. She walked to the patio door and he let her go, realizing that the hurt he'd caused her wasn't physical.

"You aren't my property," he said. "I didn't mean it like that."

She stopped and rested her head wearily against the glass door. "I am not ready for this. I am *so* not ready for this."

He moved up behind her and put his arms around her waist. Though she tensed at his touch, he took it as a good sign that she didn't move away. He buried his face in her thick hair and breathed in the scent of her. He didn't understand why being near her brought him peace, even now, when she was so agitated, but he accepted this gift she brought to his life. He hated that the last thing Sofia was feeling right now was peaceful and longed to help her.

"I'm not ready for this," she repeated in an anguished whisper.

"For us?" he asked, dreading the answer.

"For everything. For life. Everything's changed so fast. Everything is so different! I'm used to being alone, to being unwanted, to having a father who's a murderer and . . ." Her voice trailed off into a long, strangled moan.

Her tense muscles went suddenly limp, and she threw her head back with a tortured wail.

Jason quickly turned her around and pulled her close.

She shook like a tree in a storm, sobs racking her.

My father! Daddy!

I know. I know.

She cried and cried, a lifetime's worth of grief pouring out of her. She bled inside, battered by pain.

Her pain cut through him. He wanted desperately to make it stop—but no. She needed this.

Sometimes pain could be a gift, no matter what

it felt like at the time. So he held her, and loved her and waited, hoping she could come to terms with all she'd lost.

When she sagged against him, he picked her up and sat on the bed with her cradled on his lap.

After one last huge shudder, finally Sofia lifted her head. "My father went to prison for killing feral werewolves."

"Yes." Jason used a tissue to wipe her wet face.

She took the tissue from him and blew her nose. Then she scrubbed her hands across her cheeks. When he rose to carry her into the bathroom, she said, "I can walk."

He ignored her and didn't put her down until they got to the sink. He stood back while she splashed cold water repeatedly on her burning face and handed her a towel when she straightened.

"You're too good to me," she said. "I'm a blubbering fool."

"You needed the release. Feeling any better now?" He already knew the answer to that; her broken heart beat inside his body. He would do anything to make her whole.

She looked at him, her dark eyes full of bleak hopelessness. "He did the wrong thing for the right reason."

Jason nodded.

"He's serving life in Gull Bay Supermax." She swallowed fresh tears. "He did it for me." The bleak expression left her eyes, but the hurt remained.

Jason crossed his arms. "I see. You won't let yourself grieve anymore, but you will blame yourself for the choice he made. Don't do that, sweetheart. He wouldn't want you to."

"That selfless bastard," she spat out. She threw down the towel and marched out of the bathroom.

He followed her into the bedroom and watched her pace restlessly around the room. He knew a caged tiger when he saw one. An angry caged tiger.

"What are you thinking?" he asked.

She turned to him. "Can't you read my mind?"

"Sometimes it's wiser not to."

"This isn't justice," she said. "This isn't fair. What am I going to do?"

"Visit your father," Jason suggested. "Let him know you know why he did what he did. Let him know you forgive him, and that you love him."

"Of course I love him. I've hated his guts, but I haven't stopped loving him. Believe me, I tried." She went back to pacing. "I wonder if I could hire a lawyer and get the case reopened with new evidence."

"You can't mean that."

"Why not? Even if every werewolf in the world comes after me for outing them, I don't care."

"I'd care. I'd have your back, sweetheart, and I'd have to kill a lot of nice werewolves defending you."

She saw his point and kicked a chair leg in frustration, then winced. He felt the blood racing through her and the wild pounding of her heart.

"This is life and death we're talking about, Sofia. You are in my world now, and our secrets cannot be revealed."

She nodded reluctantly and began pacing again. "I know. But something has to be done! I cannot— *will* not—leave an innocent man in that place."

"He is not innocent," Jason reminded her.

She stopped moving, her fists bunched at her sides. "Why did he have to kill them? Why couldn't he have—"

"He was a father defending his child. I'd kill any monster that threatened my child."

"All right. Maybe the question is, why did he have to get caught? Where was his cleanup crew to make sure the police didn't know anything supernatural occurred?"

"That was—unfortunate."

"Something has to be done," she declared. "We have to do something to help him."

"I don't know what." He hated the way she felt, desperate and close to breaking again, her control a brittle and fragile shell. "We'll think of something," he promised.

"We could break him out of Gull Bay."

He might have laughed had this not been so deadly serious. "Sweetheart, this is real life, not some show on the Fox network."

She countered, "Vampires, werewolves, skinhead biker bad guys? Don't talk to me about *reality,* Jason Cage."

"Okay. Point taken. But how could we—"

"Wait. I think I've got an idea. Vampires. And werewolves." Sofia laughed. "It's crazy, but it just might work. Of course it'll work! It *has* to work."

He caught her enthusiasm. "What have you got in mind?"

"Do you know anything about the security at a place like Gull Bay?"

"Do you?"

"I know as much as anyone on the outside can know about Gull Bay." She shrugged. "As much as I tried to forget about my father I couldn't stop myself from doing websearches about where he is. I didn't want to know, and I couldn't bear not to."

"That is understandable."

"Is it? Anyway, Gull Bay was built specifi-cally to house Level Four offenders—the worst of the worst. It's located in an isolated spot in northern California. My father's in the Security Housing Unit, which means he spends twenty-three hours a day alone in a cell. Only the staff are allowed into the SHU, except for routine searches by drug-sniffing dogs. The dogs and their handlers are brought in from police units outside the prison. Do you see where I'm going with this?"

Jason shook his head. "No."

"You and Cathy in wolf form can go in as one of those canine units."

He began to get an inkling of what she had in mind. "You want to use our strength and tele-pathic abilities to break your father out."

She nodded. "I remember how you psychically made the cops at the motel go away. All you have to do is go into Gull Bay, make everybody in the place forget Daddy ever existed, and bring him out."

By the Goddess, the woman didn't know what she was asking! But she deserved to have her father. And he would do anything for her hap-piness. He wasn't going to tell her what it might cost him, though.

He forced a confident smile. "It's so crazy it just might work."

"Good. Let's go talk to Cathy."

When she started toward the door, he turned her around and pointed her toward the bed. "You're exhausted. I'll go talk to Cathy. You get some rest."

Chapter Forty-four

Sofia lay with her eyes closed while Jason got dressed, and she tried to go to sleep after the door closed behind him. She'd never felt so drained; her muscles burned with weariness. Yet her mind raced, and after a while she couldn't take the thoughts chasing around in her head any longer. She wanted Jason to come back and began counting the seconds he was gone.

When she grew disgusted with her neediness, she got out of bed, put a matching short robe on over her black nightgown, and went out onto the patio. A few breaths of brisk night air helped clear her head. She stared up at the beautiful night sky until she heard a footstep.

"Can't sleep?" Sid's voice asked out of the darkness. The vampire stepped onto the patio.

"Me, either. With all the psychic turmoil flying around the place, I doubt if anybody's asleep."

"You've been crying," Sofia observed.

"You, too."

Sofia nodded. "I hate living on an emotional roller coaster."

"It's been a rough week."

Sofia recalled their earlier conversation by the fountain. "I talked to Jason about fathering the baby. It didn't go well."

Sid wasn't disappointed. "That's okay. I think that plan's pretty much on hold for the moment, anyway." She looked concerned. "Did you two have a big fight over it? Is that why you've been sending out so much hysterical energy?"

"There was a bit of stress during that conversation," Sofia answered, "but my hysteria came from something else."

Sofia explained to Sid about her father, and the plan to save him. She thought Sid would be pleased by what she told her, but the vampire woman looked worried when Sofia was done.

"What's wrong?" Sofia asked. "Don't you think it will work?"

"I think that Jason Cage might be the wrong person to ask to break your dad out of Gull Bay."

Sofia was confused. "Why? He agreed with the plan."

"He's Family, and the Families have different rules about dealing with mortals than the Clans do. The Families do not directly interfere in mortal matters. He got in deep trouble for trying to save the world once already. I don't think his people will take kindly to his interfering again."

Sofia sank weakly onto a patio chair and she swore—at life, at herself. What had she done?

Totally miserable, she looked up at Sid. "I saw how determined he looked when he left. I don't think I could stop him now even if I begged him. How much trouble have I gotten him into? What do I do?"

"Talk to Lady Juanita," Sid advised. "Maybe she can think of something."

"If you're looking for Jason, he just left," Cathy said when Sofia entered the central meeting room.

"I know." Sofia tapped her forehead. "It's impossible for me not to know where he is."

There were several others in the room with her cousin. Mike and Harry Bleythin, Antonia, and David Berus were there, along with Lady Juanita and several people whose names Sofia couldn't remember.

"I'm glad you're here," Cathy told her. "We

were discussing a plan to rescue our missing relatives."

"Cathy's come up with something we believe will work," Harry said. "We want to know what you think of it."

Of course they had more than one crisis to deal with. Sofia felt almost selfish for putting her concerns first, but Jason's well-being meant more to her than anything else—even more than her father's freedom. She closed her eyes and tried to bury the pain of the loss beneath its usual layer of scar tissue.

"Are you ill?" David Berus was suddenly beside her.

"No."

Everyone's concerned attention was now on her. She tried to smile reassuringly at them, but couldn't manage it. Cathy, Mike, and Harry all came toward her, but she gestured for them to sit down.

She wasn't used to asking for help, but for once, she didn't hesitate. She looked to the Matri. "Lady Juanita, I did something that's going to get Jason in terrible trouble, and you have to help me stop him. Please."

The Matri didn't show any surprise. "But the plan to help your father sounds workable."

"After we made a few suggestions and alterations to it," Mike added.

Cathy gave Mike an annoyed look. "Mike means he insisted he be the one to go into the prison with Jason."

Mike brushed a hand through Cathy's hair. "I'm not letting my mate anywhere near a bunch of dangerous convicts. Besides, I owe Jason one."

"You don't understand," Sofia said. "Jason will be in terrible trouble if he does this. His people will punish him, and he knows it. He's being noble, which is lovely, but I can't let him go back to jail for breaking somebody else out."

"Of course, he's Family," Lady Juanita said. "He's so much like one of us that I'd forgotten the restrictions he lives under." She looked steadily at Sofia. "My dear, because he is Family and I am Clan, I have no authority to forbid him to do this."

"He's doing what's right," David said.

"His Matri won't see it that way," Mike said.

"True," David looked at Sofia sympathetically. "You and I may not approve of the way the Families choose to deal with mortals, but they have their own good reasons for their policies."

"Well, I think my uncle deserves to be broken

out of jail," Cathy spoke up. "Come on, people! Let's think of a way to get this done."

"The solution is perfectly simple," Antonia said. "Isn't it, David, my love?"

David looked at her and laughed. "I *am* Clan Prime. Rescuing mortals is what I do." He told Sofia, "I am not as strong a telepath as Jason, but my ability will suffice for the assignment. May I offer myself as the means for righting the wrong done to your father?"

Sofia's heart sang with gratitude, and she threw her arms around the big, blond vampire. "Thank you! Thank you, thank you!"

"She agrees," Antonia said. "Now get your hands off my bondmate, young lady."

Sofia quickly stepped away from David. "But what do I tell Jason? He isn't going to back off from going through with this mission."

"You need not tell him anything," Lady Juanita said. "All you have to do is go back to your room and do what comes naturally to a bonding couple."

Everyone laughed, but Sofia protested, "I can't lie to him. That wouldn't be right."

"You don't have to talk to him at all," Cathy said. "All you have to do is screw his brains out until the mission's accomplished."

"You're already dressed for it," Mike pointed out.

Sofia had forgotten she was only wearing a skimpy nightgown and robe, and she blushed. Jason had told her that the reason they kept being distracted by lust from other matters was because of the bonding. She hadn't understood at first, then the need had proved as inconvenient as it was wonderful, and now she saw how this distraction could help them. This wasn't manipulating him, it was saving him.

"All right," she told the group waiting for her decision. "I can do this."

"Bite him," Lady Juanita advised. "And get him to taste you, as well. Keep that up and neither of you will notice the time passing. Now go." She gestured toward the door. "Jason will be looking for you, anyway."

She nodded. "Yes. I'd better get him back to our bedroom, fast."

Chapter Forty-five

"I'm so sore, I don't think I can get out of bed." Sofia ran her foot up Jason's calf. "But then, I don't want to get out of bed."

She had no idea how long they'd been there. She'd hidden the clock in the nightstand drawer and had kept the curtains drawn. Time kept going in and out of focus as they made love again and again. Whenever they slept, they'd wake up to find food waiting for them, and eating always turned into lovemaking.

"Good." Jason caught her foot in his hand and started kissing her toes, which she found thoroughly erotic. He also tickled her instep, which got her giggling. The combination of sensations drove her crazy, and she became lost in them until—

"Ow! You bit my toe!"

"I did," Jason admitted, and did it again.

This time, the lightning bolt that shot through her was completely the opposite of pain.

"Do that again."

"Gladly."

He tasted her blood, and she writhed with orgasms from each little wound. When he finished with her foot, he moved to sink his teeth into the back of her leg, then to the inside of her thigh. Every touch took her higher.

His head moved higher still between her legs and his tongue began to make lazy cat laps across her throbbing, swollen clitoris. This delight took her out of herself in an entirely different sensual way, but it was no less intense. Jason's every touch brought her pleasure.

"My turn," she managed to gasp out after his tongue had worked wonders on her for a while.

He lifted his head to look into her eyes. His smile was teasing. "Sweetheart, was that an invitation?"

"It was a demand. I want to take you into my mouth."

He didn't need coaxing.

She took her time, slowly sinking her mouth onto his cock, then repeating the process again and again as she teased the swollen head and length with her tongue. She made him writhe and buck just as he had done to her, until she finally let him come.

When he was spent, she looked at him with an expression of triumph and not a little smugness. "I do believe you are wasted, Mr. Cage."

"Madam, you are wicked," he told her.

She batted her eyelashes. "I try."

"Come along." He got up and hauled her unceremoniously over his shoulder.

"Hey!" she protested as he headed toward the bathroom.

"You said you were too sore to walk."

"I said I couldn't get out of bed."

"Well, now you're out of bed." He took them into the glass-walled shower and didn't put her down until a pulsing, steaming stream poured over them. "And now you're *really* in hot water, mortal."

She picked up a thick bar of coconut-scented soap and washed his hair, then worked thick lather all over his long, muscled body. He took the bubbling bar and returned the favor, and they managed to make love standing up despite their slippery, soap-covered bodies.

When they were finally finished, Jason carried her back to the bed.

Just as he put her down, someone knocked on the door.

Jason swore, but went to answer it. She pulled on a robe and hurried after him, handing him a robe before he could open the door.

"Have you no shame?" she asked.

"None," he answered, but he did tie the belt as he called, "Who is it?"

"Lady Juanita requests your presence in the central chamber immediately," a voice on the other side of the door replied.

"Damn," Jason whispered. A Matri's request was the same as an order. He gave Sofia an apologetic look, and an affectionate pat on the fanny. "Of course," he answered the messenger.

Sofia hurried into the closet to get dressed; the eagerness that radiated from her served to clear Jason's head. He threw open the patio door curtains to discover that it was the middle of a brilliant day. He looked around the wrecked bedroom and scrubbed his hands over his face.

He remembered finding Sofia in the hallway outside the meeting room last night and their returning here. She'd said, *"I want you to make love to me as a Prime."* When she'd kissed him she bit his tongue and the sharing of blood drove him into a sexual frenzy.

That had been last night, hadn't it?

He looked at her suspiciously when she came back into the room wearing jeans and a red shirt, but she gave him such a deliriously hopeful smile, he couldn't bear to ask her what she'd done.

He had the feeling he'd find out very soon, in the meeting room.

Chapter Forty-six

Sofia barely noticed when the Prime who opened the meeting room door announced her name. The man standing by Lady Juanita's chair took all of her attention. Tears welled in her eyes and she could barely breathe.

He was taller than she remembered, and thinner. And when had he shaved his head? The wary expression on her father's face was anything but welcoming.

Instead of rushing headlong, she stopped in the center of the room and waited, awkward and unsure as silence stretched out around her.

It was Jason who finally said, "What's the matter with you, Hunyara? Don't you recognize your own daughter?" He gave her a slight shove and whispered in her ear, "He's all you want. Go to him."

Sofia was shocked into movement, more by the bitterness in Jason's tone than anything else. She began to turn to him.

Her father said, "Sofia?"

At the sound of her name, she ran forward and flung her arms around the man who'd spoken. His voice was so familiar. So was the way his arms came protectively around her.

After a while, she noticed that her embrace was just as protective of him, just as strong.

"You've grown up," he said.

She lifted her head and nodded.

"I'm sorry it was so hard on you," he said. "I didn't mean to hurt you."

"I'm fine," she said. "I really am." She looked around and saw David Berus smiling at her.

"Thank you," she said to the Prime. "I don't know how to thank you."

"The plan was yours; Michael and I merely carried it out. With your father's cooperation, of course."

"Wait a minute—" Jason began.

"I think we should leave these two alone to get reacquainted," Lady Juanita announced. "All of us," she added.

The tug of separation as Jason left was disturbing, but Sofia concentrated on her father.

"Where do we start?" she asked when they were alone.

He looked her over carefully, then met her gaze for a long time. "You're one of us," he said, and seemed disappointed.

"A Hunyara wolf tamer, you mean?"

He nodded. "I'm so sorry. All I wanted was to keep you from that curse."

She didn't feel cursed. But how could she tell the man who'd given up his freedom to protect her that he'd done the wrong thing?

"Now you're involved with werewolves and vampires, too, and the dangerous madness is going to continue through the generations."

"I can't deny it," Sofia told him. "We just have to cope. Can you—do what I do? Are you a wolf tamer?"

He shrugged. "I have the gift, though I never wanted it. I never used it after my father trained me. I passed it on to you, but I wouldn't let those old men raise my fragile little girl the way I was raised. Before your mother died, I promised her I wouldn't expose you to danger."

Well, that made sense. Mama was so girly.

"How did you learn the taming?" he asked.

"A vampire taught me." She smiled at the thought of Jason. "The same vampire who taught

Grandpa and Great-grandpa. So I've had the best teacher. I'm not afraid of what I can do. It can help people."

She explained to him about Cathy, and about everything else that had happened recently. He asked her about the years since they'd seen each other, so she told him what she'd done with her life. He didn't want to talk about life inside the prison. She supposed they'd have to probe those sore spots someday, but now was the time for happy reunions.

She had no idea how long they talked, but at some point, someone brought in a tray of sandwiches and tall glasses of iced tea. Long after they'd finished lunch, another vampire came into the room.

"Mr. Hunyara, if you could come with me, please?" he asked politely. "I'm here to help you work on your new identity, and I need to take some photos before I can go any further with the project. Sorry to take him away from you," he told Sofia as her father rose to go with him. "How would you feel about becoming a professional dog handler as your new profession, Mr. Hunyara?" the vampire asked as they left.

Sofia smiled, so grateful to the Wolf Clan for putting their well-organized resources at the disposal of her family. *I'm going to have to do something especially nice for them. Lady Juanita deserves much more than a thank-you for this.*

Once her father was gone, she remembered Jason and rose reluctantly to her feet. He was furious with her; she could feel it. No point in putting it off a moment longer.

She found Jason in the garden, sitting on the bench near the fountain. A warm breeze ruffled his brown hair. He was staring at the ground and didn't look up when he asked, "How's your father?"

His concern melted her heart. "Disoriented, I think. He's been out of the world for a long time."

"I know how that is," he said. "I'll talk to him, if you'd like."

"I'd appreciate that." She hated the strained sound of her own voice, and the hostility that was just under the surface of his. "Jason."

Blue eyes as hot as lightning suddenly met hers; the blaze of fury nearly burned her to ash where she stood.

Sofia took a step back, but fought off the urge to turn and run away. "I didn't come out here to tame a wolf," she told him.

"I'm a great deal wilder than a wolf when I let myself go." His tone was low and even, and really, really scary. "I am Prime."

"How am I supposed to translate that? Does it mean that I hurt your pride and you're pissed off at me?"

He nodded. "Very." He was standing in front of her before she could blink. "Why did you do that to me?" he demanded. "Why did you trick me while somebody else kept the promise I made to you?"

"Because I discovered how dangerous that promise was to you, and I wasn't going to let you go back to prison. I thank you for the promise. I truly appreciate your good intentions, but I had to protect you."

"It's *my* job—my duty and my privilege—to protect you, Sofia Hunyara."

"Back at you, Jason Cage," she snapped. "If we're going to have this connection between us, it has to go both ways. We have to be equals in this."

The fury slowly drained from his eyes, but his expression remained cold. "I don't know if I'm ready for this," he said. And then he left.

Chapter Forty-seven

"I can't believe he just stomped off to sulk and play with his wolves," Sofia told Cathy. "It's been three days, and I'm still upset about that conversation."

She kept her eyes on the busy freeway, trying to pretend that Jason's words didn't still sting. Every mile away from her pissed-off bondmate stretched her nerves, but this trip to Los Angeles was necessary. Maybe it was better for them to be apart, anyway.

"Men can be so melodramatic," Cathy commiserated. "He knows you did it for his own good, even if he doesn't want to admit it. Besides, it's not as if he didn't enjoy himself meanwhile—for days!"

"I hated hurting him. I should have done it a different way."

Cathy gave an earthy laugh. "How many ways did you do it?"

Erotic memories flooded her, and Sofia laughed as well. "More than I can remember."

"Jason's a Family Prime who thinks like a Clan boy. He needs to remember his pragmatic roots and learn to appreciate you."

The air conditioner in the borrowed car strained as the heavy traffic slowed. "Thanks for volunteering to help me pack up my apartment," Sofia said to her cousin.

"No problem," Cathy said. "It'll give us something to do after the vampire docs do the blood tests on us at their clinic."

"How many vampire clinics are there?"

"I have no idea. But I do know that this one in L.A. is where most of their medical research is done. I've never thought much about vampires until now."

"You had your own werewolf problems to deal with. Do you think this Hunyara werewolf-vampire connection is real?"

"I don't trust anything Eric told me," Cathy answered. "But I hope it is real, just for the sake of keeping the werewolves from coming after our Hunyara asses. Man, life has changed in the last few days! We've discovered family secrets, you got your dad back, I've got control of my shape-shifting, Mike's given up being the Tracker, and Sid's quit the firm and has gone to stay with her sire."

"Everything changes." Sofia saw the sign for their exit and moved over a lane. She sighed. "I never thought I'd drop out of college, but I posted it on my blog for the world to read about, so it must be true. So here I am, back in town to do just that. Along with a million other things."

"Blood tests and getting you moved are first on the agenda, though," Cathy said.

"So it would seem," Sofia said, and she and her cousin grinned wolfishly at each other.

"One very good thing about being a werewolf is that we heal fast," Cathy said as she removed the Band-Aid on the inside of her elbow.

"While I have a bruise the size of a quarter," Sofia complained, rubbing her arm. It felt like a half gallon of blood had been drawn by the vampire technicians. "And it itches."

"Whiny wimp," her cousin teased.

"You're buying my ice cream cone," Sofia declared as they reached the ice cream shop down the street from her apartment. There had been other medical tests, too, and the doctor who ran the clinic had asked lots of questions. They'd spent several hours there before returning to her university neighborhood. The doctor had wanted them to spend the night at the clinic, but they had other plans.

"How long before we know anything from the blood tests?" Sofia wondered as they waited in line.

"They told me several weeks, maybe months. DNA testing results really take much longer than they show on TV crime shows."

"I guess." Sofia was thinking of Jason, so she bought a double scoop of the deepest, darkest chocolate she could get.

When they had their ice cream, they went to the small park across the street. They found an empty bench under a tree and enjoyed their cones in silence for a while as they looked around the busy neighborhood a couple of blocks from the university. There was plenty of foot and car traffic to watch.

"I'm going to miss this place," Sofia said as she wiped her fingers with a napkin. "I've enjoyed school."

"Look at it this way," Cathy said. "The world loses a literature teacher and gains a wolf-taming superhero."

Sofia snorted. "I guess I can go along with that.

Except that I was majoring in electrical engineering. I read for fun."

"Whatever." A dangerous grin lit Cathy's features. "I think the bad guys read your blog and followed us to L.A. I recognize a couple of vehicles that are circling the park."

"Why, cousin dear," Sofia said as they stood. "Do you think we're about to get kidnapped?"

"I certainly hope so."

"About time," Sofia said. They began to walk toward the street. "Let's head back to my place. That ought to make it easier for them."

Chapter Forty-eight

"Good morning, ladies."

The unfamiliar voice roused Cathy to consciousness. The only scent she could detect, other than her cousin's, was that of coffee. The lack of smells told her they were in the presence of the enemy, but at least the bastards weren't complete barbarians—unless they didn't offer her a cup when she opened her eyes.

"Would you like a cup of coffee?" the man asked.

"No," Sofia answered. There was a hysterical pitch to her voice.

Cathy sat up and gave her cousin a frown. "Don't be an idiot—accept the man's hospitality."

Sofia looked their captor over carefully. He was tall and strongly built, with a long braid of blond hair and a heavy beard. His presence pretty much filled the one-room cabin.

"Not exactly a man," she corrected herself. "Werewolf."

He nodded.

"Oh, God, not another one!" Sofia had her arms wrapped around her drawn-up legs and was looking at their captor with wide, terrified eyes.

Cathy gave a disgusted shake of her head. "I bet you're Nathan," she told the werewolf. "Eric told me about you."

"Did he?" the deep-voiced male growled.

"May I have some coffee?" she asked.

He poured a mugful from a thermos and brought it to her. When she reached for the cup, he grabbed her by the hair and pulled her to her feet. "What happened to Eric?" he demanded. "What did he tell you?"

"Eric's dead," she said with a grimace of pain, leaving out the fact that she'd killed him herself. "He died when the Bleythin pack showed up to 'rescue' me. They didn't ask if I wanted rescuing," she added. "Then they made me go back to spending the moonchange locked in a cage. Eric promised me freedom. You didn't have to knock me out to get me here; I was hoping you'd come for me."

"You don't mean that," Sofia said. "You don't want to be a werewolf. *I* don't want to be one," she added in a bleak whisper.

Nathan let Cathy go and laughed at Sofia's fear. "You'll get used to it."

"You haven't bitten her yet, have you?" Cathy asked.

"No," he told her. "I'll let you do the honors to prove you really want to be part of the pack."

"Come the moonchange, I'll be delighted," Cathy said.

She didn't think he believed or trusted her for a moment, but he did finally hand her the coffee. She downed it in three gulps. "That almost helps the headache."

"Where are we?" Sofia demanded. "How did we get here?"

Cathy stood up. "Don't mind her," she told Nathan. "She's a whiny little thing who's never going to be a pack alpha." She approached Nathan. "I can see a pine forest beyond that barred window. It looks like the perfect place for our kind to run free."

He grinned. "It is."

"Why not take me for a walk?" She put her arm through his. "Show me around the place."

He didn't relax his guard, but he didn't say no. "There's food on the table," he told Sofia before leading Cathy outside. "And a guard on the door."

Once they were gone, Sofia returned to a conversation she'd been involved in since she fully awoke from the long, drugged ride. So far, she'd found out that they were being held in a large compound in a remote part of Oregon that was surrounded by an electrified fence. It was patrolled by armed guards. Their Hunyara relations and several other captives were locked up in a large central barracks, which was also guarded. The place was quite the fortress.

Am I as bad an actress as I suspect? Because Cathy's really good.

Are you sure your cousin's acting?

Please! This was all her idea. After a heavy silence filled her head for a few moments she went on, *Do not try to get me paranoid, Cage.*

All I'm saying is that sometimes you can't trust the ones you care for the—

All right, all right! I shouldn't have tricked you. How many times do I have to say I'm sorry?

Once.

Oh. Haven't I—

No.

Of course I'm sorry I hurt you. I just couldn't think of another way.

You could have asked me to let the Clan Prime go in my place. We could have talked it through.

Well . . . yeah. It didn't occur to me to be reasonable at the time. I was pretty hysterical that night. Sid said all the psychic turmoil was messing with everybody's brains.

And I've found out that Lady Juanita was messing with yours, Jason said. *Matris are born matchmakers. She saw suggesting you keep me in bed as a bonding gift to us. Due to all the blood we shared then, she pretty much arranged that we'd pass the point where we could ever leave each other.*

I don't want to ever leave you!

Nor I.

But you'd been thinking you might have to. I'd been thinking I might have to let you run off and hide with your people and stay away from you to cover your trail. We can't do that now. We didn't want to anyway.

Do you forgive me? Sofia asked. *I promise never to do it again.*

You'd better not be promising never to have an orgy again. I liked that part.

So did I. And if we want to do it again anytime soon, I suggest we get on with the rescue.

I agree. All our players are in position—even your Dad has shown up. I've been working with him on his wolf taming; he's rusty but talented.

I'm glad.

Okay, we're coming in. You and Cathy can do your thing now. See you soon.

I love you.

Love you, too. Get to work, Mrs. Cage.

Chapter Forty-nine

While talking to Sofia, Jason had been careful not to show her how worried he was for her. He kept reminding himself that she was brave and strong and resourceful, and he wanted her that way. But he would much rather lock her up somewhere safe and luxurious and keep her there. He couldn't follow those protective impulses with a wolf tamer for a bondmate, but that didn't stop him from having them.

He'd been terrified ever since he found out that she expected him to find her, no matter where she ended up or what condition she landed in. Everyone involved had assumed he'd follow the psychic trail to her, which he had. So her confidence had been well placed, but he'd still been scared he'd screw up. Now he intended to get her out of harm's way, and keep her there for as long as possible.

Coming up beside him, Mike Bleythin said, "Pashta's group is ready. Let's get this over with. I want Cathy out of there right now."

"I'm glad I'm not the only one thinking like a protective male."

"Our mates are altogether too tough for our own good," Mike answered.

Jason nodded his agreement as Laurent and Eden came up to them. The four of them gazed down from their hiding spot to the encampment below.

"I want to get my hands on the computers in there," the mortal woman said. "We need to find out what's really going on."

"I just want to kick some ass and get home to our kid," Laurent said. "Let's get moving, before the deodorant we confiscated from these jokers wears off."

"Roger that," Eden answered.

A second later, a hideous scream sounded in the compound below. They took this as their signal to move forward.

"I think Cathy's responsible for that," Mike said proudly as they ran for the fence.

The limitation to being a wolf tamer in this situation was that not everybody in this nest of dangerous lunatics would be a werewolf. When Sofia had mentioned the possibility of mortal bad guys, Cathy had come up with a solution. Everything now hinged on finding out what type of enemy was guarding her prison. Sofia stepped up to the door.

She wiped everything else from her mind and concentrated on the job at hand: she was supposed to be scared. "*Supposed* to be scared?" She managed to make herself cry and rapped on the door with both fists. "Help! Help!" she shouted. "Let me out! Somebody please help me!" She tried to mentally project that she was fragile and not a danger to anybody.

The man outside yelled for her to shut up. When she continued shouting and banging, he finally opened the door. "I told you to shut—"

She sniffled and wiped the back of her hand across her cheek. When he reached out to grab her shoulder, she looked him in the eye and latched onto a werewolf's mind. She'd taken him too much by surprise for him to put up much of a fight.

"Take me to the other prisoners," she told him.

With the guard as her escort, she crossed the compound to the barracks Jason had told her about. No one questioned their progress. When

Cathy made her move, everyone else in the compound rushed to find out what Nathan was screaming about. With this diversion under way, the attack from the outside began.

Sofia couldn't worry about the sudden gunfire from the defenders, or the huge truck that came careening down the hillside and crashed through the fence into one of the buildings. She only hoped nobody was driving it.

She had the werewolf under her control hold his weapon on her, and pretended to still be a scared captive when she went into the barracks. There, she saw five prisoners being watched by two guards. The prisoners, three men and two women, were each handcuffed to a bed frame set into the concrete floor.

"What's going on out there?" one of the guards asked. "Why'd you bring her in here?"

"You're both needed outside," her guard said, as she'd ordered him to. "Go on. I'll take over in here."

The men must have been bored, because they didn't question this order but ran out to join the excitement. Sofia hurried toward the prisoners after they left. "I'm here to rescue you," she told the staring prisoners. "If any of you is a werewolf named Hunyara, Uncle Pashta wants your help outside."

Two of the men raised their free hands, and one said, "You're cousin Sofia."

She nodded. "Help me free them," she ordered her werewolf.

He didn't have the keys to the handcuffs, but solved the problem by carefully putting a bullet through the chain on each prisoner's cuffs to break the links.

"Go to sleep," she ordered the werewolf when he was done.

She gave his gun to one of her cousins, and they went to join the fighting. "Stay here," she told the others, then ran outside, anxious to find Jason.

Once inside the compound, Jason headed straight toward Sofia. He moved too fast for any of the shooters to take aim at him, but bullets still buzzed dangerously close, hitting the dust as his feet flew by. He ignored them and happily tossed aside all those who tried to physically attack him.

Sofia's presence drew him like a beacon to the central building of the complex. She came through the doorway when he was just a few yards away, and her face lit with a smile that sent his heart soaring.

She didn't see the gunman taking aim at her.

That was all right, because Jason was on top of the shooter before he had time to fire.

When he let the body fall to the ground, Sofia looked at him with very wide eyes. "There was a time when I would have found that profoundly disturbing."

Jason grabbed her hand and took her back into the barracks, where they exchanged a quick, fierce kiss. "The operation's winding down," he told her. "Stay here until I come for you." Surprisingly, she didn't argue.

When he returned, he brought a crowd with him. Eden carried a confiscated laptop, and she and Cathy sat down to have a look at what was inside. Pashta and the other Hunyaras gathered around the three freed prisoners. Laurent and Mike stood guard over Eden and Cathy. Sofia's father stood back and warily watched everyone else, looking a bit lost amid all this activity.

Jason took Sofia aside. "You can debrief and take part later," he told her. "But first—"

Her mouth covered his, and they shared a long, lingering kiss. He held her close and she put her head trustingly on his shoulder.

"We'll have more adventures," Jason said. "But I promise you we'll always end up like this."

She looked up at him, her smile filled with joy and confidence. "Together."

"Together."

After they'd spent a few quiet moments holding each other, Jason asked, "So, how do you feel about working with animals?"

Chapter Fifty

Two months later

Sofia stood before the dressing room mirror and nervously assessed her brief, skintight costume.

George and Gracie restlessly stalked back and forth behind her, as if eager to return to the stage. The dressing room was overflowing with flowers sent by friends and family for her debut. The scent of the jasmine from Lady Juanita filled the room, blending sweetly with the yellow roses from Sid.

Jason stepped up behind her and put his arms around her narrow waist, which was emphasized by the boning in her scarlet and black costume. "How are you feeling, my beautiful lady?"

She met his gaze in the mirror. "I'm damned

glad I spent the last two months sweating with a personal trainer to get into this outfit, since I'm going to be seen in it in public tonight." Jason pulled her closer, and the reaction she picked up from her bondmate warmed her all over. "I can feel that you want to tear it off me, which isn't helping to keep me calm."

He ran his hands down her waist and around the curve of her hips. "I can't help myself. You're gorgeous."

She thought *he* was the gorgeous one, with the skintight pants that showed off his muscular thighs and the open white silk shirt that revealed his chest and emphasized his broad shoulders. It was enough to make her limbs go weak with lust—if they weren't already weak from stage fright.

"I'm going to be jealous when we go out there and all the women start screaming." The moment of truth was nearly here and Sofia was scared to death. "I was crazy to agree to this after your assistant e-mailed that she and her new husband had decided to buy a boat in Bora-Bora and sail around the Pacific. Anyone could have replaced her onstage."

"But it is a good job opportunity for you here in dull, mundane Las Vegas."

She smiled shakily. "Only a vampire would call Sin City dull and mundane."

"A vampire and a wolf tamer, you mean." He hugged her close again. "You and I know what *real* excitement is. Once you're onstage, it will be easy."

She had to admit, this should be much easier than chasing down evil werewolves bent on world domination. Since she'd begun rehearsals with Jason, her father had stepped into the role of main Hunyara wolf tamer.

"Did your father decide to come?" Jason must have sensed her thoughts.

She nodded. "Along with every Hunyara that Cathy and Uncle Pashta could dig up. I've learned that we used to be circus people. So in a way, I'm returning to my roots with this job."

"All of the Bleythins and many from the Wolf Clan are also in the audience to cheer you on."

"I'm delighted. But Sid sent her regrets from Los Angeles. She and Joe still aren't talking, by the way."

After an embarrassed moment, he asked, "Did she find a sire for—"

"Yes. I don't know the details though."

"And I don't want to know them." Jason turned her to face him. "I'm afraid I'm going to mess up your beautifully applied lipstick, my love."

A knock on the door and a call of "Ready for you" stopped him from kissing her. They touched noses instead.

"Come along, Mrs. Cage," he said, taking her hand to lead her to the stage. "The tigers are waiting."

Pocket Star Books
proudly presents

PRIMAL HEAT

Susan Sizemore

Now available
from Pocket Star Books

Turn the page for a preview of
Primal Heat. . . .

"Not more Queen," a man said behind her.

The disgust in his voice amused her, and the deep British accent was intriguing. As the band played "Another One Bites the Dust," she took the water the bartender handed her, then turned around. She hadn't seen the man standing behind her before, though she was somehow already aware of his presence before he spoke. His hair was wavy and sandy brown, his eyes green and surrounded by laugh lines. He had a lived-in face; a dangerous face.

"I know what you mean," she told him. "If they play 'Fat Bottomed Girls,' I'm out of here."

"I'll join you," he answered.

"And, if they play a lot of Def Leppard, Jo will probably run away screaming."

The newcomer followed Phillipa as she edged around the dance floor toward the terrace.

"Who's Jo, and what's wrong with Def Leppard? I'm a proud son of Sheffield myself," he added. "Same hometown as the Lep—"

"Wait. What do you mean, *who's Jo?*" Phillipa stopped and confronted him. "You *are* a guest at the Elliot-Cage wedding, aren't you?"

His smile was devastating, showing deep dimples and crinkling the lines around his eyes. "I'm the best man."

Irritation flared over the heat that had been roused by his smile. "You're Matt Bridger! You very nearly ruined this wedding!" she accused.

"It's not my fault my plane was late."

"You were supposed to have arrived yesterday."

He gestured at the boisterous people filling the crowded room. "It doesn't look like I was missed."

"One of my brothers stepped in as best man."

"Then it all turned out all right." He crossed his arms over his wide chest and moved close to her. "I don't know what you have to be angry about."

"I'm angry on my sister's behalf."

"Why's that?"

"She's Jo Elliot."

"The singer in Def Leppard?"

"The bride!"

Even as she indignantly stepped closer, Phillipa realized that Matt Bridger was teasing her.

Suddenly they were toe to toe and nose to nose. He put an arm around her waist, drawing her even closer. She was caught by the masculine heat and scent of him. "You're provoking me on purpose."

The back of his hand brushed across her cheek. "Yes."

Her knees went weak, and she almost dropped her glass. She didn't notice where it went when he took it out of her hand.

"Dance with me."

"Yes."

Of course. She never wanted to dance with anyone else.

He drew her onto the dance floor, and they started slow-dancing to the fast music. It was the most natural thing in the world to gaze into this stranger's eyes and press her body against his, soft and hard blending. They didn't share a word while the music played, yet the communication between them was deep and profound. She'd known him forever, been waiting for him forever. It was all too perfect to make any sense.

When the music stopped she would've kept right on dancing, but Matt Bridger turned them off the dance floor. Her arms stayed draped around his wide shoulders, and her gaze stayed locked on his. His palms pressed against the small of her back, large and warm and possessive.

Despite this intimate closeness, Phillipa tried to regain her sanity.

"We've just met."

"And you're really not that kind of girl."

"What kind of girl?"

"The sort who snuggles up to a stranger the moment they meet. And I'm not that sort of man." He flashed that devastating smile at her again. "Mostly."

"Then why are you and I—"

"We have more than snuggling in mind."

"Yes, but—"

"I have a theory."

She didn't want to hear his theory. "Kiss me."

Fingers traced across her lips. "Soon."

His touch left her sizzling. This was crazy! She should be embarrassed.

She took a deep breath, and made an effort to step away. She managed to move maybe an inch, making it a small triumph for public decency.

"Like calls to like," he said, pulling her back to him.

She lost interest in decency. "I'm a cop."

"Fancy that." As the music started again, he took her by the hand. The connection was electric. "Come on."

She held back. This was her last chance to stay virtuous. "I don't—"

"Listen."

She did, and laughed. "Oh, my God, 'Fat Bottomed Girls.'"

"You said you'd leave if they played it."

"Left alone with big fat Fanny—"

"Matt Bridger, let's get out of here."

They headed toward the door, but he stopped after a few steps. "One thing, first."

"What?"

"Your name."

"Phillipa Elliot."

Now, at least, she wasn't about to fall into reckless abandon with a *total* stranger.

He tilted his head and gave her a quick, thorough once-over. What he saw was a tall blond woman in a strapless, tea-length teal satin bridesmaid's dress.

"I know, I don't look like a Phillipa," she said. "But who does?"

"Pardon me for saying so, but that is an unfortunate name for a Yank, isn't it?"

"I'm used to it."

"Good. It suits you."

The band started to play louder, and they ran for the door.

"That was—" Phillipa sighed, unable to describe the experience. Now she understood why sex was called "the little death." Maybe it was just *great* sex that was called that.

Little sparks of pleasure were still shooting through her; she was exhilarated and exhausted at the same time. She was completely content to lie across Matt, her breasts pressed against the hard muscles of his bare chest. She rested her cheek against the warmth of his skin and breathed in the male scent of him.

"It certainly was," Matt answered.

She glanced up to see his hands propped behind his head, a smug smile curving his beautiful mouth. She caught the sparkle of green in his half-closed eyes.

"You look like a well-fed cat," she told him.

"Very well-fed," he answered. "But still hungry."

He pulled her up the length of his body for a kiss. His mouth was as insistent and needy as if they hadn't just made love. He made her hungry all over again. His hands began to roam, and her body responded.

This time she was able to keep her head long enough to say, "Maybe we shouldn't." His mouth circled a nipple. "Oh God! I mean—there's supposed to be photos—and—wedding stuff." Her mind was too into the pleasure to remember just what. "We'll be missed."

He nuzzled her, and his voice came muffled from between her breasts. "Do you really care?"

"Nooo—yes! We'll be missed. I should be there. She's my sis—" She suddenly became very aware of his erection, and her hand closed around it. She *had* to touch him, to stroke him. "I shouldn't be doing this."

"You better not stop."

His hungry growl sent a needy shiver through her. His voice was enough to make her melt. "But—"

This sort of thing happens at family gatherings all the time.

"What happens?"

People disappear to make love. It's a way to celebrate the bonding.

"That's nice." It occurred to Phillipa that there was something odd about this conversation. "Did you just say something inside my head?"

Not that you'll recall. Relax, sweetness. Make love to me.

"All right." It was all she wanted to do anyway.

As a carousel version of "Ode to Joy" woke Phillipa, she thought, I belong with this man. When she came a little further awake, she realized that the noise was a cell phone ringing, and that she was lying naked in a dark hotel room with Matt Bridger. She couldn't think of anywhere better to be, and snuggled closer to him while Beethoven kept playing.

Eventually Matt rolled over and picked the phone up from the nightstand. "Mike, if you're drunk, you're a dead lobo."

Whatever the answer was, it made Matt sit up. His muscles bunched with tension. "Where and when? Right. I'm not alone."

Deciding to let him ride out this emergency in privacy, Phillipa slid out of bed and crossed the dark room to the bathroom. There she took her time using the facilities and drinking a glass of water.

Even as she stepped back into the bedroom, she was aware of the emptiness. The musky tang of sex was still in the air, but even before she turned on a light and saw the rumpled, empty bed, she knew he was gone.